MOTHER
KNOWS BEST

Mother Knows Best

A Fiction Book
by
Edna Ferber

Short Story Index Reprint Series

BOOKS FOR LIBRARIES PRESS
FREEPORT, NEW YORK

CONTENTS:

STANDARD BOOK NUMBER:
8369-3338-9

LIBRARY OF CONGRESS CATALOG CARD NUMBER:
77-110187

PRINTED IN THE UNITED STATES OF AMERICA

Contents

Mother Knows Best

MOTHER
KNOWS BEST

Edna Ferber

MOTHER KNOWS BEST

THEY say there never was such a funeral in the history of New York's theatrical life. Belasco was there, and of course Dan Frohman; and though it was an eleven o'clock funeral, even two of the Barrymores got up in time to arrive at the undertaker's chapel just before the casket was carried out. The list of honorary pallbearers sounded like the cast of an all-star benefit at the Century. And as for the flowers! A drop curtain of white orchids; a blanket of lilies-of-the-valley; a pillow of creamy camellias; sheaves of roses; banks of violets. Why, the flowers alone, translated into money, would have supported the Actors' Home for years. Everything was on a similar scale. Satin where others have silk; silver where others have brass; twelve where ordinarily there are six. And her mother, Mrs. Quail ("Ma Quail"—and the term was not one of affection), swathed in expensive mourning which transformed her into a sable pillar of woe through whose transparencies you somehow got the impression that she was automatically counting the house.

In the midst of it all lay Sally Quail, in white chiffon that was a replica of the full floating white chiffon dancing dress that she always wore at the close of her act. A consistent enough costume now. Sally was smiling a little; and all those telltale lines that she had fought during the past ten years—the tiny lines that, between thirty and forty, etch themselves about a woman's eyes and mouth and forehead—were wiped out magically, completely. What ten years of expert and indefatigable massage had never been able to do, the Mysterious Hand had accomplished in a single gesture. You almost expected her to say, in that thrillingly husky voice of hers, and with the girlish simper that she had adopted when she went on the professional stage at fourteen and still had used—not so happily—at forty:

"I will now try to give you an imitation of Miss Sally Quail at twenty. Miss . . . Sally . . . Quail . . . at . . . twenty." And it had then turned out to be an uncanny piece of mimicry, embodying not only facial similarity but something of the soul and spirit as well. Though in this particular imitation, according to the Scriptures, soul and spirit were supposed to have fled.

Crushed though she was by her sorrow, it had been Ma Quail who had seen to it that this, her talented daughter's last public appearance, should be, in every detail, as flawless as all her public appearances had been. A born impresario, Ma Quail. During the three days preceding the funeral she had insisted that they come to her for sanction in every arrangement, from motor cars to minister. And she supervised the seating arrangements like a producer on a first night.

"Sally'd have wanted me to," she explained. "She always said Mother knows best."

Of course a lot of people know that Sally Quail's real name was Louisa Schlagel. Not that it matters. Even a name like that couldn't have stopped her climb

toward fame. The Schlagels, mother and daughter, had
come from Neenah, Wisconsin, propelled rapidly by
Mrs. Schlagel. Between Neenah, Wisconsin, and Chicago, Illinois, they had become Mrs. Quail and Sally
Quail, respectively. Mrs. Schlagel had read Hall Caine's
The Christian. Both book and play of that name were
enormously in vogue at the time. She had thought the
heroine's name a romantic and lovely-sounding thing
and had, perhaps almost unconsciously, appropriated
its cadences for use in her daughter's stage career.
"Glory Quayle . . . Glory Quayle. . . . Sally . . . Sally
Quayle . . . Sally Quail. . . . that's it! Sally Quail. That's
short and easy to remember. And you don't run into
anybody else with a name like that."

There's no doubt that if it hadn't been for this tireless
general and terrible tyrant, her mother, Sally Quail
would have remained Louisa Schlagel, of Neenah,
Wisconsin, to the end of her days. Though her natural
gifts had evidenced themselves even in her very early
childhood, it had been her mother—that driving and relentless force—who had lifted her to fame and fortune.
That force of Ma Quail's, in terms of power units
—amperes, kilowatts, pounds—would have been sufficient to light a town, run a factory, move an engine. The
girl had had plenty of spirit, too, at first. But it had been
as nothing compared to the woman's iron quality. If
ever a girl owed everything to her mother, that girl
was Sally Quail. She said so, frequently. So did Ma
Quail.

Sally was forty when she died of typhoid after an illness of but a few days. You were a little startled to

learn this. Somehow, you had never thought of her as a mature woman, perhaps because she had never married, perhaps because of her mother's unceasing chaperonage. All her life she was duennaed like a Spanish infanta. Through her mother's tireless efforts Sally Quail had had everything in the world—except two things.

In announcing her death the newspaper headlines called her Our Sally. The news was cabled all over the world, and was, certainly, as important in London and Paris as in New York and Chicago and San Francisco. Hers had been international fame. Hundreds of thousands of people were conscious of a little pang born of shock and regret when they said, over the morning paper at breakfast:

"I see where Sally Quail's dead. Gosh, that's too bad! She was just a kid. First time I saw her was in—let's see —no, she couldn't have been so young, at that. Must have been darned near forty. But an artist, all right. They say she got five thousand a week every time she stepped into vaudeville. . . . Say, look here, this coffee's stone cold again. Why is it you can't get a hot cup of coffee in this house!"

When Ma Quail was Mrs. Schlagel she had been the wife of Henry Schlagel, than whom there was nothing in Neenah less important. He was a small druggist of the kind who doesn't install a soda fountain in his drug store. Even Mrs. Schlagel couldn't make a success of her husband Henry, though she had early turned the full battery of her forces upon him; had tried to bully, bribe, cajole, threaten, nag, scold, and weep him into it. She was a fiercely ambitious woman, but there was no moulding Henry. He was fluid, spineless. When you tried to shape him he ran through your fingers. Henry came of better stock than she. Mrs. Schlagel had sprung from a rather common lot living the other side of the tracks. Her marriage with the meek and dusty little apothecary had been, technically, something of a social triumph for the girl. Her father had been a day labourer, her mother a slattern. The girl, lively, high-spirited, good-looking in a bold dark sort of way, decided to lift herself out of this and did it in ten visits to the fusty little drug store on fictitious errands. The little pharmacist, mixing drugs and grinding powders between mortar and pestle, knew nothing of the mysteries of human chemistry. His marriage was as much a surprise to him as it was to the rest of the town.

The girl Louisa was born fully six years after their marriage. By the time she was six years old the mothers of the neighbourhood knew just where to find their off-spring any summer evening after supper. They were certain to be gathered under the corner arc light with the June bugs blundering and bumping blindly all about and crackling under foot, while Louisa Schlagel recited "Little Orphant Annie" and sang "Jolly Old St. Nicholas" (with gestures) and gave imitations of the crowd's respective papas and mamas with uncanny fidelity. Stern parental voices, summoning children to bed, died away unheard on the soft summer air. Or, if heard:

"Willie! Clara! Come on now!"

No answer.

"Will Meyers, don't you let me call you again!"

"Well, Pete's sake, wait a minute, can't you. She's in the middle of it."

Sometimes an irate parent would come marching down to the corner bent on violence, only to be held in thrall.

It was absurd, because she was a plain child, thin, big-eyed, sallow. By the time she was twelve she was speaking pieces at the Elks Club Ladies' Evening and singing and giving imitations at church sociables and K.P. suppers. The little druggist objected to this, prompted by something fine and reticent within him. But his wife was tasting the first fruits of triumph. She had someone to manage, someone to control, someone on whom to turn the currents of her enormous directing energy. By the time Louisa was thirteen her mother was demanding five dollars a performance for her services, and getting it, which was in its way as much of a triumph in that day and place as was the five-thousand-a-week contract which she consummated in later years. At thirteen the girl was a long-legged gangling creature, all eyes and arms and elbows and (luckily) soft brown curls. She had no singing voice, really, but the vocal organ possessed a certain husky tonal quality that had in it something of power, something of tragedy, much of flexibility. And when she smiled there was something most engaging about her. A frank, boyish sort of grin that took you into her confidence: that said, "Aren't we having a grand time!"

It is difficult to say how her mother recognized the gold mine in her. She induced the manager of the little local vaudeville theatre to let Louisa go on one Monday night in an act made up of two songs and three imitations and one dance that was pretty terrible. It was before the day of the ubiquitous motion picture. The Bijou presented vaudeville of the comic tramp and the Family Four variety. Sandwiched in between these there appeared this tall gawky girl with terrifically long legs and a queer husky voice and large soft brown eyes staring out from a too-thin face. The travelling men in the audience, hardened by the cruelties of Amateur Nights in vaudeville, began to laugh. But the girl finished her opening song and went into her imitations. She imitated Mansfield, Mabel Hite, and Rose Coghlan, all of whom her mother had taken her to see at the Appleton Wisconsin Opera House just twenty-five minutes distant by interurban street car. The one-night stand was flourishing then, and the stars of the theatre were not so lofty that they would refuse to twinkle west of Chicago. Well, even the travelling men saw that here was a weird and unusual gift. Something in the sight of this awkward white-faced child transforming herself miraculously before their eyes into the tragic mask of the buxom Coghlan, or the impish grotesqueries of the clownish Hite or the impressive person of Mansfield moved the beholder to a sort of tearful laughter. Still, it cannot truthfully be said that there was anything spectacular about this, her first appearance on a professional stage. The opinion was that, while the kid was clever, she ought to be home in bed.

That trial served to crystallize into determination the half-formed plan in Mrs. Schlagel's mind. She took the child to Chicago, lied about her age, haunted such book-ing offices as that city afforded, hounded the vaudeville managers, fought the Gerry society, got a hearing, wrote her husband that she was not coming back—and the career of Sally Quail was started.

To the day she died there always was something virginal and untouched looking about Sally Quail. It was part of her charm. At twenty she looked seventeen. At twenty-nine she looked twenty. At thirty she looked twenty-five. At thirty-five she looked thirty—under that new overhead amber lighting. And then, at thirty-nine, suddenly, she looked thirty-nine. Though she was massaged and manicured and brushed and creamed and exercised and packed in cotton wool she took on, in some mysterious way, the appearance of the woman of whom we say that she is well preserved.

For twenty-five years—from fifteen to forty—nothing could prevent Sally's progress, for the way was cleared for her by her mother. That remarkable woman pushed on as relentlessly, as irresistibly as a glacier, sweeping before her every obstruction that stood in her path. Here was this girl who could sing a little, though she had no voice; dance a little, though she had too long legs; act a little, though her dramatic gift was slight; mimic marvellously. No one ever made more out of little than did Ma Quail. She fought for contracts. She fought for plays. She fought for a better spot always in vaudeville, and even from the first Sally never closed the show. It was years before Sally became a real headliner in vaudeville, with the star's dressing room and her name in electric lights over the entrance. But her mother surrounded her with all the care, the glamour, the ceremony of stardom. She was tireless, indomitable, in-escapable. Press agents featured Sally just to escape her mother. Office boys wilted at her approach. Managers and producers received her with a kind of grim and bit-ter admiration; recognizing this iron woman as one against whom their weapons were powerless.

"Now, look here, Mrs. Quail," they would say, in desperation, "you don't expect me to go to work and star a girl that hasn't got the stuff for it." Then, in an-ticipation of what was coming, from the look in Ma Quail's face, "Now, wait a minute! *Wait* a min-ute! I don't say she won't, after a while. Give her time. She's only a kid. Wait till she has a little experience. She'll grow. Prob'ly be a great artist some day. She's a great little kid, that kid of yours. Only——"

Though it was, perhaps, old Kiper himself speaking, here he floundered, hesitated, stopped. Ma Quail's steely glance ran him through. "Only what?"

A heartening champ at his unlighted cigar. "Well—uh—how old is Sally now? Between us, you know. I mean—how old is the kid?"

"Nineteen."

"Hm. Twenty-one, huh. Ever been in love?"

Ma Quail bridled. "Sally has always had a great deal of attention, and the boys all——"

"Ye-e-e-s, I know. I know. Has she ever been in love?"

Mrs. Quail pursed up her lips, bridled, tossed her head. "Sally is as unspoiled as a child, and as pure as one, too. She's never even been kissed. She——"

Ben Kiper brought one fat fist down on the mahogany

of his office desk. "Yeh, and why! No fellah's going to kiss a girl when her mother's holding her hand. Now, wait a minute. Don't get huffy. I'm telling you something for your own good, and nobody knows better than Ben Kiper that when he does that he loses a friend every time. But I'm going to tell you, just the same. You've been a wonderful mother to that kid, but if you're smart you'll let her alone now. Let her paddle her own canoe a little. Give her a chance. What if she does run on the rocks a little, and bump her nose and stub her toe——" He was getting mixed in his metaphor, but his sincerity was undeniable.

"You're crazy," said Ma Quail. "Sally can't get along without me. She's said so a million times, and it's true. She can't get dressed without me, or make up. She can't go on unless I'm standing in the first entrance. She'd be lost without me."

"Yeh. Well." He made a little gesture of finality, of defeat. "All right, Ma. You win. Only, when she leaves you, don't come around and say I didn't warn you."

Ma Quail stood up, her diamond ear-drops flashing with the vigour of her movements. She had started to buy diamonds in Sally's second year of stage success. At first they were rather smoky little diamonds of the kind that cluster around a turquoise for support. But as the years went on you could mark the degree of Sally's progress by the increasing whiteness, brilliance, and size of Ma Quail's gems. She bought them, she said, as an investment. At this moment they were only fair in size, refractive power, and colour. But they took on life from the very energy of their wearer.

"And let me tell you this, Mr. Kiper. When the day comes that you'll offer my Sally twenty-five hundred a week, and she'll turn it down——"

"You'll turn it down, you mean," interrupted Kiper.

"All right. I'll turn it down. But just remember the time when you refused to star her for five hundred a week. You can tell the story on yourself if you want to. You're probably just fool enough."

Which is no way for a stage mama to talk to a powerful and notoriously kind-hearted old theatrical manager. But as it turned out, he was wrong and she was right, in the matter of predictions.

Ben Kiper, seeing that he had hit home, decided he might as well let Ma Quail have both barrels and make an enemy for life. He was interested in Sally's career and fond of the girl. And he was a wise old gargoyle. Ma Quail was fastening her furs, an angry eye on the door. Kiper fixed upon her a look at once patriarchal and satyric—in itself no mean histrionic feat.

"Now, listen, Ma. You know's well as I do that no girl can make a hit in musical comedy unless she's got sex appeal. And how's anybody going to find out whether Sally's got it or not until you cut loose those apron strings you've got her all tied up with? My God— a stage nun! That's what she is. Let her fall in love and break her heart, and pick up the pieces, and marry, and have a terrible time, maybe; and fight, and make up, and get——"

Ma Quail was at the door. She looked every inch the stage mother. Suddenly her face was darkly stamped and twisted with jealousy and fear. "Sally doesn't want to marry. Sally doesn't want to marry. She's told me so."

"Yeh?" The old eyes, with the oyster pouches beneath, narrowed as they regarded her. Freud and fixations were not cant words at that time; and certainly old Ben Kiper foresaw nothing of the latter-day psychology. But he knew many of the tortuous paths that twist the human mind; and here he recognized something familiar and ugly. "Yeh? Who put that funny idea in her head? Give her a chance, why don't you?"

"If my Sally ever marries it'll be a prince."

"Prince! Hell! Not if she picks him," yelled old Kiper, just before she slammed the door behind her.

You would have thought that blunt talk like this might have opened her eyes, but such scenes only served to increase Ma Quail's watchfulness, her devotion, her tireless planning.

Sometimes headliners (feminine) used to resent the pomp and ceremony with which Ma Quail would surround this young person who was only filling third spot on the vaudeville bill. A change of costume in the wings. A velvet curtain hung there for protection. A square of white sheeting on the floor before the emergency dressing table so that the hem of her gown should not be sullied; a wicker clothes basket, chastely covered with snowy white, holding her quick change—gown, slippers, make-up. A special pan of special resin in which to rub the soles of her satin slippers before she went into her dance.

"Listen! Who's headliner on this bill—me or Quail?" they would demand of the house manager.

Mother and daughter went to the theatre together. Ma Quail stood in the wings throughout the time that Sally was on stage; dressed her; undressed her; made her up; criticized her; took her home. Put her to bed. She brought her her breakfast in the morning. They ate their early dinner together; their bite of late supper. Sally was an amiable and generous girl, and devoted to her mother. But there were times when she was unaccountably irritable, restless, impatient. Ma Quail put this down to temperament and was rather pleased than otherwise.

Sally's big chance in musical comedy (*Miss Me* ran two solid years in New York) did not come until she was twenty-four. Before she was starred in that success she had won solid recognition in vaudeville, and in musical comedy rôles that were not stellar. And always, just ahead of her, her mother, inserting a wedge here, getting a toe in there, widening the opening that led to stardom.

It was when Sally was playing the old Olympic Theatre in Chicago that Ma Quail fell ill and was forced to take to her bed. It was influenza, of which there was a particularly violent epidemic at the time. It was elegantly termed "la grippe"; or, as Mrs. Quail explained, "a touch of the la grippe." She literally had never been ill, and thought that, by treating this illness with contempt, she could vanquish it. For one afternoon and one evening performance she stuck it out, appearing sunken-eyed and putty-faced at the theatre, there to stand alternately shivering and burning in the wings until finally they forced her to go back to her hotel (they were stopping at the old Sherman House) and to bed, where she just escaped pneumonia. They got a nurse, though Ma Quail fought this.

Sick as she was, and even a bit delirious the first twenty-four hours, she still ruled Sally from her bed. Sally was playing down on the bill, which meant a good spot toward the end of the programme in the second half. Ma Quail fumed until Sally was off to the theatre; tossed and turned and muttered during her absence; began to listen for her return a full hour before the girl could possibly have finished her act. She thrashed about on her pillows, sat up, threatened to get out of bed, quarrelled chronically with her long-suffering nurse, was as impatient and difficult as a sick man.

"Now she's putting on her make-up. She never gets it on right unless I'm there. Chunks her grease paint. . . . Now she's dressing. There was a hook that was working a little loose on her white. It may be off by now, for all I know. I should have caught it when I noticed it, but I thought I'd do it next. . . . Now it's almost time to go on. That Nixon is just ahead of her. I told them not to run those two acts next to each other. Not that that cheap hoofer's act is anything like my Sally's. But she ought to follow a sketch. If I was up I'd make them shift the bill. . . . Now she's on. . . ." She would hum a little tune, her eyes bright and heavy with fever, a dull glow in her sallow cheeks, her hair twisted into a careless knot on top of her aching head. . . . "That's right. That's right. Go on. . . . Now she's off. There's her bow music. She's taking her curtains. One . . . two . . . three . . . four—she could have had another if they'd taken the curtain up again. . . . She'll be home now in half an hour . . . twenty minutes . . . fifteen . . . ten. . . . What time is it, Miss Burke?"

The long-suffering Miss Burke would tell her the truth, having tried a professionally soothing lie on her first day with Ma Quail, and having been caught in it, with effects not calculated to allay fever in a case of la grippe.

"Now, Mrs. Quail, you mustn't get yourself all worked up this way. Just see if you can't drop off a minute before Miss Sally gets back. She'll be here before you know it, and then won't you be surprised!"

"Talk like a fool," retorted Ma Quail. "What's keeping her, I wonder."

On the first day of her mother's illness Sally tore off her clothes, only half removed her make-up, flew back to the hotel, sat by her mother's bedside against the nurse's warnings and the half-hearted protests of her mother. The second matinée she returned to the hotel directly after her performance, but her haste was, perhaps, a shade less feverish than it had been the night before. On the third night, after she had finished dressing, she came out to the first entrance and stood there to watch Nixon doing his act. Nixon was the hoofer of whom her mother had spoken with contempt. His act preceded hers. Ma Quail never permitted Sally to stand in the entrance watching the other acts. "Keeping tabs," it was called; or catching the act; and Sally loved to do it, particularly when the act was a dancing act. She loved dancing, especially clog and soft shoe. At both of these Nixon seemed to be expert. Curiously enough, she found three pairs of eyes squinting through the tiny gap in the old red plush curtain that hung before the first entrance. High praise, certainly, for Nixon. Three —and now, with Sally, four—fellow actors on the bill keeping tabs on his act meant that Nixon's act was worth watching.

"New stuff?" whispered Sally to the nearest ear.

"Every time he goes on. Wait a minute. There now. Get that one. He didn't pull that one this afternoon. He makes every other hoofer I ever saw look like they was nailed to the floor."

Sally, standing in the entrance, applied a fascinated eye to an inch of slit in the curtain. Involuntarily the muscles in her long nimble legs ached to do these incredibly difficult feats that seemed so simple to the uninitiate. Nixon did a black-face single. His act was that of a dancing monologist, so that Ma Quail was justified in thinking that he should not have preceded Sally. His monologue was dullish stuff; his dancing nothing short of marvellous. His was perfect muscle control, exact rhythm sense, and an assumption of indolent ease in motion that carried with it a touch of humour. Sally had been on dozens of bills with him; knew him as a shy and quiet young man who called her Miss Sally and crushed himself up against the wall to let her pass; a decent young man, descended from a long line of hoofers; a personable enough young man with a lithe waist, a quick smile, white teeth, and a Midwestern accent. Born, he said, in Kansas City, but the world was his address. His costume—to which his black face lent the last touch of the ridiculous—was an exaggeration of the then fashionable male mode: peg-top trousers, wide silk lapels, saw-edged sailor, pointed shoes. In contrast with this grotesquerie he seemed, off-stage, all the more shy and, somehow, engaging and boyish.

As he bounded off now, went on again for his bows, off, and turned toward the passage that led to his dressing room, Sally, ready to go on, forgot her own invariable nervousness in her interest at what she had just seen and envied.

"Where did you get that one?" She tried to do it. They were playing her cue music. It was time for her to go on.

"No," grinned Nixon, very earnest and polite behind the black smear that was his make-up. "Go on. You take 'em. I'll show you."

He was waiting for her when she came off—a thing that had never happened to her before. Trust Ma Quail for that.

"But I don't want to steal your stuff," Sally protested.

"Say, I'd be proud to have you even look at it, let alone want to catch it. Leave me show you how it goes."

"Mother's sick."

"Yeh. I heard. Say, that's too bad. How is she?"

"She's better, only she gets nervous if I don't come straight back to the room soon's I'm dressed. But maybe —just five minutes——"

They observed the proprieties by leaving her dressing-room door wide open. "Now look . . . . Naw! . . .Naw! . . . Look! One and two and three and slide and *turn* and one and two and three and slide and *turn* and . . . looka what I do with my knee there . . . See? Naw! . . . Stiff.

. . . That's it! You'll get it. Only you got to practise. I bet I was three months at it, mornings, before I put it in."

You got a mental picture of him, in dancing trunks, in his grubby hotel bedroom, solemnly and earnestly mastering the intricacies of this new step, his stage a carpet that had been worn gray and threadbare by many dancing mirthless feet.

Sally meant to tell her mother the cause of her delay. She didn't dream of not telling her. After all, she had picked up a new dance step. But when she reached her mother's room she found there a woman in such a state of hysteria, brought on by anxiety and general devilment, that she heard herself, to her own horror, making up some tale about having had her spot changed—moved down on the bill—a change for the better. She felt stricken at what she had done. Then she realized that she would have to do it again to-morrow—and next day—and the next—and the next. And suddenly a vista—not a wide one, but still a vista—opened out before her mind's eye. An hour to herself every day. Every day—an hour—to herself. She did not say this, even to herself. She did not even think she thought it. Something seemed to say it for her. She did not even think of a way to explain her explanation, should her mother recover before the end of the week. But she wouldn't be able, surely, to come to the theatre before the end of this week's bill. Sally hoped she would, of course—but she wouldn't.

Sally came out of the stage entrance after her afternoon performance that next day and stood a moment on the top step blinking almost dazedly at the dim, slimy, dour Chicago alley. It looked strangely bright to her, that alley; a sort of golden light suffused it. An hour. She had an hour. As she stood there, blinking a little, she was like a prisoner who, released after long years of servitude, stands huddled at the prison gates, fighting the impulse to creep back into the cold embrace of the gray walls that have so long sheltered him. So Sally thought, "Well, I guess I'll go right home."

But she didn't. Instead she began to stroll in a desultory manner down Clark Street, looking in the windows. She was conscious of a sensation of exhilaration, of buoyancy. That sordid thoroughfare, Clark Street, took on a fascination, a sparkle, a brilliance. Sally saw in the window of a candy store a great square pan of freshly dipped dark brown chocolate creams. She went in and bought a little paper sackful. Her mother rarely allowed her to eat sweets. They were bad for her complexion. Sally now strolled on down the street, consuming her plump chocolates by a process as unladylike as it was difficult. You bit off the top of the cone-shaped sweet, or, if you preferred, you bit a small opening at the side, taking care not to make this too large, and including in this bite as little as possible of the creamy fondant beneath. This accomplished, the trick was to lick at the soft white filling with a little scooping flick of the tongue, much in the manner of a cat consuming a saucer of cream. Little by little, thus, the fondant melts on the tongue, disappears, leaving a hollow shell of chocolate, an empty cocoon. So Sally Quail, in her new freedom, strolled exulting down Clark Street, staring into the windows, stopping before some of them, her little pointed red tongue working busily away at the sweet held in her fingers, her face beatifically blank as the sugary stuff trickled down her grateful throat. There was even a little unsuspected dab of chocolate on one cheek, near her mouth. It gave her a most juvenile and engaging look.

She was thus engaged when Nixon approached her, breathing a trifle rapidly, as though he had been running. She showed, queerly enough, no surprise at seeing him. He fell into step beside her.

"I didn't see you go out. I was getting dressed. You must've jumped into your clothes."

"Blm," said Sally, companionably, her mouth full of fondant; and held the sack out to him, hospitably. He took one, ate it, took another, ate that, suddenly noticed her method, which she was pursuing calmly and without affectation.

"Say, that's a great system you got, Miss Sally. How'd you like to have one six feet high, and lick your way right through it!"

Sally laughed heartily at this, and so did he, though it wasn't very bright. And so, still giggling, they reached the Sherman House. And a little stricken look of contrition came into Sally's face. He said, "Well, so long. See you to-night. Uh—say, there's a little spot of chocolate on your cheek."

"Where?" And rubbed the wrong place.

"Right—there." He whipped out a handkerchief, put it back hastily, took out another, neatly folded, and held it up, hesitating. "If you don't mind——"

She didn't mind. He rubbed it off, gently. There was something intimate, something protective, about the act.

"See you to-night, Miss Sally."

"See you to-night."

On the way up she gave the remaining chocolates to the elevator boy. And then the usual questions, the usual answers. How many curtains? How much applause? How was the house? Was the headliner still high-hatting her?

The evening show.

Nixon wanted to introduce a song into his act. No, he couldn't sing, he told her. Not what you'd call sing. But you know. One of those coon songs. Kind of fresh up the act. He asked her advice about it. He hung on her answer. Her decision. Sally Quail, for whom everything was decided. Sally Quail, who never was allowed to do anything for anyone. Everything done for her. No one allowed her to do for them. Not her capable martinet mother, surely. It was sweet to have someone dependent on you for his decision; someone who thought your advice valuable—not valuable only, but invaluable. She was riding straight for catastrophe, was Sally Quail, without ever being warned of the road.

They watched each other's act, matinée and evening. She was there just the moment before he went on—that moment when the vaudeville actor "sets himself" for his entrance. She had seen them do all sorts of things for luck to last them through the concentrated fifteen minutes of an act. She had seen them cross themselves. She had seen them rub a tiny talisman. She had seen them mutter a prayer. Nixon, sprung from a long line of acrobats, black-face minstrels, hoofers, always went through a little series of meaningless motions before the final second that marked his entrance music. There was a little preliminary cough, a shuffle, a backward glance over his shoulder at nothing, a straightening of the absurd hat, tie, coat; a jerk at the coat lapel, a hunch of the shoulders, a setting of his features—all affording relief for strained nerves. Click! He was on, walking with that little exaggeration of the Negro shuffle, his arms hanging limp and loose and long, his eyes rolling tragically. He had rehearsed his new song and now he tried it out at the close of his act. It was one of those new coon songs and was called I Guess I'll Have To Telegraph My Baby. It was the type of plaintive comic that preceded the Jazz Blues of to-day. He had, really, no more of a singing voice than Sally. But he had a plaintive tonal quality, and a melodious resonance that caught and held you. He got two extra curtains on it, thus cutting in on Sally's act time. She did not resent this, though when he came off he apologized with something resembling tears in his eyes.

"Why, say, I didn't go for to crab your act, Miss Sally. Why, say, I wouldn't have done that for the world. Why, say——" He was incoherent, agonized.

Sally, set to go on, looked up at him. No girl of experience would have shown unconsciously the look that Sally turned upon him. Certainly her mother had never seen that look in her eyes. Her face was sparkling, animated, glowing. Dimples flashed where dimples had not been. In that look you saw pride in the achievement of someone else—someone for whom she cared. She even said it.

"Don't be silly! I'm proud of you. Glad you stopped the show." And went on.

If Ma Quail had been there it would have taken the house manager, the stage hands, firemen, ushers, and doorman to hold her.

Ma Quail, in her hotel bedroom, had impatiently endured five days away from the theatre; five days without seeing her Sally go on; five days of domination by a nurse. The nurse left, always, at eight. This evening, as Ma Quail lay there, fuming, she was racked by a feeling of unrest, of danger to Sally. She had had that feeling before, and nothing had come of it. It was due, of course, to her unwholesome absorption in the girl, though she would not have admitted this even if she had recognized it as being true. The feeling grew, took complete possession of her. Sally was in the theatre. Sally was dressing; Sally would soon be going on. She could endure it no longer. Trembling and dizzy with the peculiar weakness that even a brief siege of this particular illness leaves, she dressed shakily, catching at chairs and tables for support. She took a carriage to convey her the short distance to the Olympic. Sick and shivering as she was, she actually seemed to take on a new strength and vigour as she passed the stage doorkeeper. She sniffed the theatre smell sensitively, gratefully. For years it had been incense in her nostrils. Sally would be almost ready to go on, now that her act had been shifted to a spot down on the bill. She actually resented this advantage having come to Sally without her mother having fought for it. Up the winding iron stairway; down the narrow dim hall; a smile of anticipation on her face. She turned the knob of Sally's dressing-room door; she opened the door softly, softly, so as to surprise her Sally.

Sally Quail, with her head thrown back, was looking into the eyes of Jimmy Nixon, of the Dancing Nixons. Nixon's arms were close about her. Sally's eyes were half closed. Her chin was lifted with shy upward eagerness. Her mouth was tremulous and ripe and flexible—the lips of a woman who knows that she is about to be kissed. It was a kiss she never received.

"I love you, Sally," said Nixon.

And, "Oh, I love you, too," said Sally Quail. Her voice was a breath, a whisper.

There was something terrible, something indecent about Ma Quail's ruthless tearing apart of these two young things. She did it so horribly, so brutally. Her jewel was being stolen. The flower that she had tended and nurtured was being plucked by clumsy alien hands. Ugly words bubbled to her lips and broke there.

"Get out of here!" She slammed the door, advanced menacingly. She actually seemed about to strike him. "Get out of here you—you cheap hoofer, you! Get out or I'll have you thrown out!" She turned to the girl. "You fool! You little fool!"

Nixon unclasped the girl, but he still held her hand in his. As always, under emotion, he spoke the slow and drawling tongue of the born Kansan.

"You can't talk thataway to us, ma'am."

Sally said nothing. Her face was white and drawn and

old. The sight of it whipped Ma Quail into fresh fury.

"Can't!" she spat out in a whisper that had all the vehemence of a scream. "I'll can't you! Get out of here, you bum, you! I'll have you thrown out of the circuit. I'll fix it so you'll never show in any decent house again. I'll—"unconsciously she used a term she had heard somewhere in cheap melodrama—"I'll break you!"

He grinned at that. He took a step toward her, drawing the frightened girl with him. "Come on, Sally," he said quietly. "Come on away out of here."

"I'm afraid," whispered Sally. "I'm afraid. Where?"

"You know," he said. "What we were talking about. Nixon and Quail."

But at that, of course, Ma Quail fainted for the first time in her life. And when she had been revived she insisted that she was dying, and Nixon had been sent out of the room, and they took off her stays, and rubbed her hands and gave her whiskey, and she rolled her eyes, and groaned, and made Sally promise, over and over, that she would never see Nixon again. It was her dying wish. She was dying. Sally had killed her. And of course Sally promised, racked by self-reproach. And that was the end of that, and, everyone will admit, a good thing for Sally.

Ma Quail prevailed on the management to retain Sally's act for another week, which broke up contact with Nixon in the next week's bill, scheduled for Milwaukee.

Sally probably forgot all about it in later years. Curiously enough, she never would talk about it, even to her mother. And though the prince her mother was expecting never came, practically everything else in life did. Fame, and fortune, and popularity, and friendship. A house in London, a house in New York, an apartment in Paris. Private trains. Perhaps no woman of the theatre ever made (honestly) such fantastic sums as Sally Quail earned yearly for twenty years. Under her indomitable mother's shrewd management she became polished, finished, exquisite in her art, though she managed, somehow, miraculously, to retain something of her girlishness and simplicity and lovableness to the end. Still, sometimes if you glimpsed the two driving on Fifth Avenue or in the Bois, you wondered about Sally. You saw them driving in one of those long low foreign cars that are almost all engine. One of those cars that proclaims the fact that its owner has at least two others. You know. It had a hood over the back, but no hood in the front, so that the chauffeur and a good half of the delicate upholstery were unprotected. It was a proud and insolent car that said, "I am a bibelot. I am a luxury. I am practically no good at all except when the sun is shining—but not shining too hotly. When it is fair, but not too cool. I am only to be used at special times by special people. I am the specialest kind of car for people who don't have to care a damn. I am money. Look about you. You won't see many like me."

Sally looked none too glowingly happy in the hooded depths of this gorgeous vehicle, a luxurious fur rug tucked about her gifted knees, a toy dog sticking his tongue out at passers-by in lesser cars.

Sally Quail's tragic and untimely death broke her

mother completely—or almost completely. Small wonder. Still, she derived a crumb of comfort from the touching and heartbreaking last moment that preceded Sally's going. In the midst of the fever that consumed her she had what seemed to be a lucid last moment just before the end. Ma Quail told of it, often and often, over and over, to sympathetic friends.

For at the end, as she lay there, looking, in her terrible illness, much much more than her forty years, suddenly her face had assumed the strangest look—the look of a girl of twenty. There was about it a delicacy, a glow. She sat up in bed as though she were strong and well again. All the little lines in her face were wiped out queerly, completely, as though by a magic hand. She lifted her chin a little with a shy upward eagerness and her fever-dried lips took on the tremulousness and the flexibility of the lips of a woman who knows that she is about to be kissed. Her arms were outstretched, her eyes fixed on something that she found wonderful and beautiful.

"Sally!" Ma Quail had screamed. "Sally! What is it! What is it! Oh, my God! Look at me. It's Mother! Mother loves you!"

And, "Oh, I love you, too!" said Sally Quail. Her voice was a breath, a whisper.

EVERY
OTHER
THURSDAY

EVERY
OTHER THURSDAY

Edna Ferber

EVERY OTHER THURSDAY

FROM the moment she thrust a swift and practised arm from beneath the bedclothes to choke the seven o'clock alarm, Helmi was suffused with the thought that it was Thursday. Not merely Thursday, but *Thursday*. Not only that: it was *every other Thursday*. And every other Thursday was Helmi's day out.

She lay there, snug, under the welter of gray blankets, savouring the delicious thought. Her mind leaped at one bound over the dull hours that intervened between 7 A. M. and 2 P. M. From two on and on, the day lay before her, sparkling, golden, new minted, to spend as she liked. She had it planned, down to the ultimate second.

A pioneer April fly buzzed drowsily at her tightly closed bedroom window. Here in America people slept with their windows wide open, but Helmi knew better than that. The night air is poisonous, as anyone can tell you. Helmi never opened her windows until the really hot June nights set in—sometimes not even then. Habit is strong; and there had been no steam-heat in the Finland farmhouse of her girlhood, and Finnish nights are cold.

Next Sunday was Easter. At Easter time, one year ago, she had had no new hat, no new dress, no new coat, no new strapped slippers like the rest of New York. Last Easter she had been thankful just to be here.

33

Lonely and homesick, but thankful. This Easter would be different. This very afternoon would find her in One Hundred and Twenty-fifth Street East, which is New York's uptown Finland. There she would buy a blue dress and a bright blue silk hat such as Lempi Parta had worn at the Finnish Progressive Society hall last week; and pale tan silk stockings, and strapped slippers.

For more than a year a great slice of her wages had gone to pay back her brother Abel Seppala and her brother's wife Anni for the money they had sent her to buy her passage over—her two passages over. Those terrible two passages, the first unsuccessful, so that she had seen New York's sky-line approach and recede; the second dramatically successful. She could laugh now when she thought of that successful second landing. They had fooled them, all right, that time. It had cost one hundred and twenty-five dollars the first time, and one hundred and fifty to bribe the steamship steward the second time. Helmi had been almost a year and a half paying back that money to Abel and Anni.

This afternoon she would go to Anni's, in Brooklyn, as usual. But not to stay. From there she would take the subway quickly to One Hundred and Twenty-fifth Street. She had so many things to do. So many lovely things. She ought to start before two, or how could she do all these things that must be done? That must be done to-day because it would be two weeks before Every Other Thursday came again. Perhaps she would let her off at half-past one, or even one, if the work was finished . . .

The sound of water rushing into the tub in the bathroom off Their Bedroom. Mr. Mawson! He had to have his breakfast at twenty minutes to eight, sharp. It was quarter past seven! Helmi leaped out of bed, flung off her sturdy cotton nightgown, dived into the knitted union suit, the faded tan silk stockings with a run down the seam of one—discarded of Miss Zhoolie—the old sateen petticoat, the blue gingham work dress. Into the stuffy little bathroom off her bedroom. A dab at her face, a splash with her hands, a hasty running of the broken comb through her bobbed pale yellow hair (that bob had been the first step in her Americanization). Helmi always combed her hair after she was fully dressed. It was interesting to hear Mrs. James G. Mawson on that subject, among others.

Out to the kitchen. Bang! The coffee-pot. Rattle! The spoon. Slam! The ice-box door. Clash! The silver. Clatter! The china. Whiff-whoof! The swinging door. Three breakfasts to get at three different times, and the front room to be tidied in between.

Mr. Mawson had his breakfast in the dining room at twenty minutes to eight. James G. Mawson (the Mawson Optical Company) was a silent, grayish, neat man, behind glasses with special lenses. His breakfast never varied. Half a grapefruit or a glass of orange juice. Two four-minute eggs. Two pieces of whole wheat bread, toasted. A cup of coffee. Two lumps of sugar. Plenty of cream. Out of the house at five minutes to eight.

In March he had essayed to diet. Mrs. Mawson had said he was getting paunchy, and decreed but one piece of toast, thinly buttered; black coffee with no sugar; one egg. For two mornings he had obediently sipped his coffee, though with a wry face, and had left half of it, a sable pool of bitterness, in his cup. Mrs. Mawson never breakfasted with him. The third morning he broke an oblong of sugar in half and slipped the piece into his coffee. The fourth he just tinged the blackness with one small splash of cream. The fifth Helmi brought him two pieces of toast. He ate them both. The sixth she prepared two eggs as usual, placed the sugar and cream at his hand, and left the room.

These men in America! These husbands! Poor spineless things, treated like little boys by their wives and daughters. In Finland it was different. The women were independent, yes, like the men. But the men were not bossed by the women. These two women, they ran him. Do this, do that, go here, go there, I want thus, I want so. He hardly ever rebelled. Sometimes, but not often. Usually he just looked at them in silence, and a little line would come into his forehead. Between Helmi, the Finnish maidservant, and Mr. James G. Mawson of the Mawson Optical Company, there existed an unspoken and unsuspected sympathy and understanding. Helmi spoke rarely. She was an almost inspired cook.

Miss Zhoolie always dashed into the dining room just before nine in a frantic rush, and gulped her orange juice standing, in hat and coat. Mrs. Mawson's voice would be heard from her bedroom. "Zhoolie, you eat something hot before you go out."

"I can't. I've got a nine o'clock. I'm late now."

"I don't care how late you are. . . . Then get up ten minutes earlier. . . . Then don't stay out until one. . . ."

If it's only a cup of hot coffee. . . ." But Miss Zhoolie had gone to her class at Barnard.

The Mawsons lived in Eighty-sixth Street West. Those lessons to which Miss Zhoolie dashed each weekday morning were in One Hundred and Sixteenth Street, Helmi knew. Evidently in this country it made no difference if you reached these classes on time or not.

Mrs. Mawson's tray you brought to her bed every morning at nine, after the others had gone. It was quite a hearty breakfast, considering that Mrs. Mawson Wasn't Strong. She could not rise for breakfast because this brought on one of her headaches. She always spoke of these afflictions in the possessive. One of my headaches. It was as though she cherished them.

It was not hard, once you had got the hang of it. A year ago she could never have done it, but Helmi learned quickly. She had had to work much harder than this on the farm in Finland; had worked in the fields, not only from dawn to dark but far into the bright northern summer nights. Still, this was hard in a different way. Here they were always changing things, doing things differently after you had learned to do them in one way. In Finland the work had been set, inevitable. Now the cabbages, now the rye, now the potatoes, now the corn, now the oats. The horses, the cows, the sheep, the pigs. But here you never knew. With Mr. Mawson you knew. But not with Her. And not with Miss Zhoolie. Often, after they had told her to do a thing one way and she had learned it that way, they changed their minds and told her to do it another. But Helmi went ahead and did it in the original way, disregarding them. Mrs. Mawson said she didn't understand her.

"I must say I don't understand that girl. Really, she's a closed book to me. You can't be friendly with her. She just looks at you. Her face is like a joss-house idol. I honestly think she could come in and find us all murdered and weltering in our blood and she wouldn't turn a hair—especially if it happened to be her Thursday."

The conversation was between Mrs. Mawson and her nineteen-year-old daughter Zhoolie. Zhoolie had been christened Julia, after the departed distaff grandmama. This, in her fourteenth year, she had Latinized to Julie, which she insisted on pronouncing as though it were spelled with a Zh and a double-o. It must even be stated that she frequently even signed herself thus, especially in the tenderer branches of her Barnard educational career.

James G. Mawson spoke up unexpectedly, as he sometimes did when they thought he had not been listening. "Mighty good girl just the same," he said. "Knows her business and minds it."

"Helmi's a teep," said Zhoolie.

"A what?" inquired James G. Mawson, over the top of his newspaper.

"A teep."

"Spell it."

"T-y-p-e, teep. That's French."

"Well, you," retorted Mr. Mawson, "make me seek. S-i-c-k, seek. That's English."

Sometimes Zhoolie was driven to referring to Helmi as that Hunky. This usually when Helmi had succeeded in making an important (to Zhoolie) telephone message more than usually unsolvable. Her thick tongue and un-accustomed ear made a sorry business of these com-munications. "W'at? . . . Yeh, iss . . . Who? . . . Yeh. . . . She ain't here. . . . Wait, I write. . . ."

Mrs. Mawson on her return home, or Zhoolie, would find a scrawl to the effect that someone named U-J-B-D-M had telephoned, and had asked her to call up as soon as she got in. Helmi's own telephone communica-tions were as mysterious as they were private, being carried on in a guttural flood of Finnish, to Mrs. Maw-son's bafflement. She always had a helpless feeling that she was being talked about.

Helmi would never make a modish-looking maid. Hers was a trim enough figure, in a broad-hipped, ample-bosomed, wide-shouldered peasant sort of way. But you always felt that her neat afternoon uniform of black and white confined her against her will, and that some day she would rend these garments from her in a furious burst of Nordic freedom. This irked Mrs. Mawson and Zhoolie.

"Still, if you have only one maid, what can you do? Of course"—hastily—"the Woman comes in to clean one day a week, and the Wash Woman. But Zhoolie has so many friends. Half the time Helmi isn't present-able when people come to the door. And her room!" Mrs. Mawson would then gather the subject into a neat bundle and tie it with the sinister generality that they were all alike.

Helmi's bedroom undeniably was not the most ex-quisitely kept of bowers. Perhaps, after daily scouring, dusting, mopping, and wiping the rest of the Mawson apartment, there was a certain wholesome and nicely balanced defiance shown in the slightly musty disorder of her own private chamber. After all, your chef develops a personal indifference toward food; and walking is no treat for a mail carrier.

Mrs. Mawson had a way of investigating this room on Helmi's Thursday out. This she excused on the ground of housewifeliness. The room was always the same. On the lower shelf of her table reposed last summer's white shoes. There they had been throughout the winter. On her dresser a little mound of spilled talcum; a torn hair net; photographs of bridal couples in cataleptic attitudes, and family groups as stiff as woodcuts; a Sunday rotogravure picture of a motion-picture actress and an actor. Stuck in the sides of the dresser mirror were coloured picture post cards that caused both Mrs. Mawson and Zhoolie some merriment. These were, they thought, pictures such as a six-year-old child would cherish. Done in crude greens and reds and pinks, they depicted an old man, white-bearded, got up like a Santa Claus in a pine forest; a white-robed princess-looking female floating on a wave, with stars and sunbursts shooting all about her; a brown bearded man hammering at a forge like the Village Blacksmith. At the top of these pictures was printed the word Kalevala. Underneath, in finer print, unpronounceable words like Wainamoinen and Ilmatar and Joukahaimen.

"Some Finn fairy tale, don't you think?" Zhoolie said. "Poor thing. I'd like to take her up to school for a mental test. Outside her cooking and housework I'll bet she'd make an average of a child of eight."

Certainly Mrs. Mawson and Zhoolie never knew that the Kalevala is the national epic of Finland; the "Paradise Lost," the Shakespeare of that northern country; and that its rhythms, well-known to Helmi and studied by her in her girlhood at the excellent Finnish country school, had been borrowed and stolen and copied by many a versifier included in Zhoolie's English course at Barnard. Zhoolie would have been startled if she could have translated the cadences of the thumbed and greasy volume that lay on the table shelf beside Helmi's last summer's shoes.

> On his back he bound his quiver,
> And his new bow on his shoulder,
> In his hands his pole grasped firmly,
> On the left shoe glided forward,
> And pushed onward with the right one,
> And he spoke the words which follow . . .

"My goodness, *why* doesn't she open her windows! And look at her lovely bedspread that I took such—*why* do they always sit on the edge of the bed and never on a chair! And just see this bathroom. I am simply going to tell her that she must bathe oftener than—— Oh, they're all alike!"

Always capable and energetic in a slap-dash, lunging kind of way, Helmi, on this particular Thursday in April, was a tornado. There loomed ahead of her the regular Thursday routine which, on Every Other Thursday, was a rite. The kitchen linoleum must be made spotless. There was some American superstition about the sink faucets being left shining on Thursdays out. On the other hand, it was understood that lunch—if

any—was to be most sketchy on Every Other Thursday;
that Mrs. Mawson would go out for this meal if possible.
Zhoolie never lunched at home on week-days. Helmi
was free to go when her work was finished.

These things had come to be taken for granted, tacitly.
There was little conversation between mistress and
maid. Helmi practised the verbal economy of her race.
She spoke rarely, and then in monosyllables. Yeh, iss
... I bake a cake wiss nuts. ... What you want for eat?
... The iceman, the butcher boy, the grocer, the janitor,
the service-elevator boy, in person or at the telephone,
got short shrift from Helmi in any case. On Thursdays
she was curt to the point of insult. Strangely enough—or
perhaps not so strangely—this indifference to their ad-
vances gave Helmi a certain desirability in their eyes.
When occasion presented itself they attempted to woo
her in the *patois* of their kind.

"Say, you're a sketch. You hate the men, don't you?
I bet the guy gets you'll have a right to wear a umpire's
mask, all right. Listen, baby, don't you never go nowheres? How about a movie? Don't you dance or nothing?"

Did she dance? Did she dance! For what else did she
live! To what other purpose was Every Other Thursday
planned! Ask the girls and boys at the Finnish Progressive Society hall in One Hundred and Twenty-sixth
Street. Especially (alas!) the girls; the girls who
swarmed there on a Thursday night with their half-
dollar clutched tight in their big capable palms. You
went to these dances alone. If you were popular you
danced with the boys. Otherwise you danced with the

girls. By half-past eight the big dance hall on the top
floor was comfortably filled. By half-past nine it was
crowded. By half-past ten it was packed. The heavy-
handed band boomed and pounded out the fox-trot, the
waltz, the German polka. Did she dance? Did she
dance! These American boys were fools.

This Thursday night she would dance in her new blue
dress to be purchased on One Hundred and Twenty-
fifth Street. In her new tan silk stockings and her new
strapped slippers. And then perhaps Vaino Djerf would
dance with her. Helmi danced very well indeed. She
knew that. She had been the best dancer in her district
in the old country. She had noted how Vaino watched
her as she danced at the hall on Thursday nights.

But her clothes! It was not for such as Vaino to dance
with her. Vaino, of all the Finnish chauffeurs, drove the
finest car. It was big like a railway locomotive. It had
great lamps like barrels, and glittering with silver.
Often you saw this gorgeous vehicle outside Progressive
Hall where Vaino took his pleasures—his Finnish steam
bath, played pool, danced, boxed in the gymnasium.
But when Helmi had her new clothes it would be different. He would dance with her then. She would talk to
him (not much—but just enough to let him know that
her people in Finland were not common farmers; that
she had read the Kalevala; had gone to school; could
figure; was a superb cook; owed nothing more on her passage money and could save from now on).

There! Mr. Mawson had almost finished his breakfast.
Miss Zhoolie's orange juice on ice. A good half-hour in
which to start the cleaning. She attacked the living

room with fury. Ash trays. Papers. Plump the cushions. The carpet sweeper. Dust.

Usually she accomplished all this almost noiselessly. It was understood that Mrs. Mawson must not be disturbed. But this morning she need not be so careful, for Miss Zhoolie's voice, energetic in argument, and Mrs. Mawson's plaintive tones could be heard in unaccustomed early morning dialogue. Zhoolie was in her mother's room, and dressing frenziedly as she talked.

"Well, you can ask her. . . . Well, Pete's sake, we do enough for her. . . . But I didn't know until last night. Jane asked me if I'd have them to-night instead of Saturday because they're going to Atlantic City on Friday, all of a sudden. And she's been so wonderful to me, and you know what it means on account of Len. Let her go out to-morrow instead of to-day. My gosh! It isn't as if she really did anything! Goes and squats at her sister's or whatever it is, in Brooklyn, and drinks coffee. . . ."

"Sh-sh-sh-sh!" Then Mrs. Mawson's voice, dulcet, plaintive. "Helmi! Helmi, will you come here just a minute?"

Helmi pretended not to hear; made a great to-do with her carpet sweeper. Wasn't it Every Other Thursday? Did not every minute count? Zhoolie opened her mother's bedroom door, poked her head out, called sharply, but with the edge of the sharpness illy concealed in a false sheath of velvet.

"Helmi, Mother wants to speak to you just a minute, please."

Helmi leaned the handle of the carpet sweeper against

the table and came. Mrs. Mawson was in bed. She looked very plain and showed her age. Helmi, nineteen, wondered how it must feel to be as old as that; felt a stir of sympathy. In spite of the long period of passage-money payment, she had monthly sent money to her mother in Finland. It was well for Mrs. Mawson's peace of mind, and pride, that she could not read Helmi's thoughts behind that flat Finnish face. Miss Zhoolie stood in the background. She was fastening her blouse with absent-minded expertness. Little vibratory electric sparks of suspense seemed to dart out from her to Helmi.

Mrs. Mawson cleared her throat ever so slightly; pursed her mouth into the semblance of a placating smile.

"Helmi, Miss Zhoolie just learned last night that the guests she was expecting for dinner on Saturday night—three, you know—Mr. Mawson and I were going out—there were to be four, with Miss Zhoolie——"

"Oh, Mother, do come to the point."

"Miss Zhoolie wants to know—they can't possibly come on Saturday—they're leaving town unexpectedly on Friday"—a sound from Zhoolie—"wants to know if you can't stay in to-day so that they can come to dinner to-night—she's to let them know this morning—and take Friday out instead. Will you do that?"

"No," said Helmi.

The monosyllable was so flat, so final, so direct that it had the effect of stunning her hearers slightly; they appeared not quite to understand. Mrs. Mawson actually repeated, painstakingly, as though Helmi had not grasped her meaning: "You could have to-morrow, Friday, instead of to-day. You probably have no plans.

And it looks a little like rain anyway to-day, don't you think?"

"No," said Helmi.

"You mean no, you won't? Or——" Then, at the look on Zhoolie's face: "I'll tell you what, Helmi! You could take this Sunday instead. Easter Sunday. It isn't your Sunday, but you could have it——"

"No," said Helmi.

Zhoolie remained in the background no longer. She stamped her foot. Colour suffused her pretty face. "Well, I think you're a mean thing, Helmi! What have you got to do but go and sit at your sister's——"

"Zhoolie!"

"It's true. She hasn't."

Mrs. Mawson fixed her smile again, but not very successfully. It was really only pasted on, and crooked at that. "To tell you the truth, Helmi, one of the young men coming is someone Miss Zhoolie is very—she likes especially, do you see? And that's why she wanted them particularly to-night. This young man . . ."

This young man. Helmi turned and looked at Zhoolie in her soft girlish beige jersey frock, and her silk stockings, and her smart tan strapped slippers. Her young man! Well, let her get him, then. Helmi had the getting of a young man to see to. So they stood staring at each other, these two girls; Helmi nineteen, immovable, inscrutable, implacable; Zhoolie nineteen, lovely, tearful, spoiled, furious. Helmi's thoughts, translated, would have read: "Get your young man, if you want him. I have seen your young men, and a poor lot they are, too. I would not exchange my Vaino for a half-dozen of them." Zhoolie's flashing eyes and trembling lips meant: "Great clumsy Hunky! To think that you can actually spoil my day for me—maybe my life! Oh, damn! Oh, damn!"

Aloud she said again, "But, Helmi, it isn't as if you really had anything special to do. What do you do on your Thursday out that you couldn't do on Friday!"

What did she do on her Thursday out that she couldn't do on Friday! Within herself Helmi smiled and hugged her golden day to her. The Finnish girls uptown. Lempi Parta. Blue dress. The Finnish steam bath. Swim. Supper. The play at Finnish Hall. The dance. What did she do on Thursday that she couldn't do on Friday! She looked at Zhoolie, unmoved. She looked at Mrs. Mawson, her mistress. Looked at her stubbornly.

"No," said Helmi. Turned, and went back to her work in the living room; went back with redoubled and more furious energy to make up for precious time lost.

"I don't *care!*" cried Zhoolie, like a child. "She's a nasty mean thing. What does she do! Nothing! Not a thing. She hasn't the intelligence to plan a holiday. She hasn't a thing to do."

Up the hall came Mr. James G. Mawson on his way to the Mawson Optical Company downtown. He glanced in at the bedroom door. "What's the row?" he asked. "What's the row?"

"Oh, nothing," said Mrs. Mawson wearily. "I can feel one of my headaches coming on."

Zhoolie turned a tear-stained face to her father. "I want Helmi to take to-morrow out instead of to-day, and she won't."

"Don't blame her," said James G. Mawson, maddeningly.

"Oh, you're always like that, Father! Abe Lincoln stuff. It's one of your poses. What difference does it make what day she takes out, anyway!"

"Not any difference to you, Julia; might make a lot of difference to her . . . Well . . ." The front door slammed behind him.

"I've heard people say 'cold as a fish,'" observed Mrs. Mawson. "'Cold as a Finn,' I'd say."

Helmi consumed little enough food as a rule, aside from copious and unlimited cups of coffee and hunks of rye bread. Mrs. Mawson bought rye bread studded with caraway, just for Helmi. In citing Helmi's virtues Mrs. Mawson was wont to include this. "She really doesn't eat a thing, I'll say that for her. I don't know what she lives on. Eating and bathing seem to be two habits that have never got much of a hold on Helmi."

To-day Helmi ate even less than usual. She swept through the house like a Juggernaut—living room, bedrooms, dining room, kitchen. By noon she had done the work of three women; had done all the work there was to be done. A cup of coffee taken standing at the kitchen table. By twelve-thirty the smell of burning hair pervaded the Mawson flat. Mrs. Mawson had not yet gone out. She sniffed the air with an expression of extreme distaste. She walked down the hall to the kitchen. Helmi, fully dressed, of course, in her street clothes except for her coat and hat, was heating her curling iron at the gas stove.

"Not finished with your work already, are you, Helmi?"

"Yeh."

"Everything?"

"Sure."

"The ice box?"

"Thursday iss no ice box. Saturday iss ice box."

"Oh—well . . ." Mrs. Mawson drifted vaguely away.

Helmi made her final trip with her curling iron from the gas stove to her bedroom mirror. It was not yet one o'clock as she sat stolidly in a subway train marked Brooklyn. Seeing her, you would have known her for a foreign-born servant girl on her Thursday out. High flat planes of cheek bones; low full breasts; broad shoulders; pale blue eyes; frizzed bobbed hair; a pretty good cloth coat; silk stockings; a velvet hat. Certainly you would never have guessed that golden hours filled with high adventure lay ahead of this lumpy creature; and that an exciting and dramatic year lay behind her.

Helmi Seppala was being slowly digested in the maw of New York. Her passage money had been sent her by her brother, Abel Seppala. She had sailed from Abo. New York reached, she had been turned back at Ellis Island. Her country's quota was already filled. The thing had been overwhelming. Months passed. Again Abel sent money, against the protests of his wife Anni. This time Helmi bribed the steward on the ship, and sailed as one of the stewardesses. One hundred and fifty dollars that had cost. How sick she had been! She was racked now at the thought of it. The boat reached New

York. Unforeseen red tape bound Helmi to the ship. The stewardesses were not allowed to land. Frantic, she managed to get word to Abel.

The boat remained five days in New York. On the day it was due to return to Finland, Abel and Anni came on board, ostensibly to bid farewell to a Finnish friend who was going to his home country. Concealed, they carried on board with them American-made clothes—a dress, a coat, shoes, a hat, powder, rouge, eyeglasses. These had been smuggled to Helmi. Feverishly she had shed her uniform, had put on the American clothes, the rouge, the powder, the eyeglasses. When the call had come for visitors to go ashore, Helmi, with Abel and Anni, had passed down the gangplank under the very eyes of the chief steward himself—to the dock, to the street, into the amazing spring sunshine of a New York May morning. Spurned as an alien by her stepmotherland, she had disguised herself as a native daughter and achieved a home that way.

At once she had gone to work. At once she had gone to school. Anni had not been very cordial to this sister of her husband. But she had grudgingly helped the girl, nevertheless. She had got her a "place." The wage was small, for Helmi knew no English and was ignorant of American ways, of New York household usances. But from the first, part of that infinitesimal wage went to pay back the passage money loaned her by Abel and Anni. And from the first she had gone to night school, three nights a week. Three nights a week, from eight until ten, after her dinner dishes were washed, she attended the night-school class, sitting hunched over a

scarred school desk used by fourth grade children in the
daytime. It was a class in English for both sexes.

Most of the women were servant girls like herself—
Swedish, Finnish, Czech, Latvian, Polish, Hungarian.
She had had the look of the Old Country. A big-boned
girl, with broad shoulders and great capable hands.
She had worn her hair pulled away from her forehead
and temples, held with side combs, and wound at the
back in a bun of neat, slippery braids. In her ears she
wore little gold hoops. Her hair was straw-coloured,
with no glint of gold in it; her eyes blue, but not a deep
blue. She was not pretty, but there had been about her
a certain freshness of colouring and expression. Her hair
clung in little damp tendrils at the back of her neck.
There was great breadth between her cheek bones, her
shoulders, her hip bones. Her legs were sturdy, slim, and
quick. She listened earnestly. They read out of a child's
reader. The lesson was, perhaps, a nature study.

"What is a frog, Miss Seppala?"

Miss Seppala would look startled, terrified, and un-
comprehending, all at once.

Again, articulating painfully with tongue, teeth,
palate: "What—is—a—frog, Miss Seppala?"

Much gabbling and hissing from those all about her.
Suddenly a great light envelops Miss Seppala. She
bounces up.

"A frock iss an animal wiss legs iss jumping all the
time and iss green." Triumph!

The lesson went on to say, "Dragon flies are called
darning needles." Miss Speiser, the blonde, good-
natured, spectacled teacher, spoke upper West Side New

York English. "Aw dawhning needles hawmful?" she inquired. The result was that Helmi's English accent turned out to be a mixture of early Finnish and late Bronx most mystifying to the hearer. Still it had served.

And now, a year later, her hair was bobbed, and her clothes were American, and she said, "I'll tell the vorld," and got twenty dollars each week at the Mawsons'. She had paid back her passage money down to the last cent, so now Anni, in one of her tempers, could never again call her a dirty Lapp—that insult of insults to the Finn or Swede. She had learned with amazing swiftness to prepare American dishes, being a naturally gifted cook. She knew how to serve from the left, to keep the water glasses filled, not to remove the service plates until the dinner plates were at hand, to keep thumb marks off glass salad dishes, to mix a pretty good Bronx cocktail. She was, in short, an excellent middle-class American servant—spunky, independent, capable, unfriendly.

It was a long trip from West Eighty-sixth Street to Finntown, in Brooklyn, where Abel and Anni lived. Helmi begrudged the time this afternoon, but she went out of a sense of duty, and custom, and a certain tribal loyalty. Anni's house was a neat two-story brick, new, in West Forty-fourth Street, Brooklyn. The neighbourhood was almost solidly Finnish. The houses were well kept, prosperous-looking, owned by Finn carpenters, mechanics, skilled workmen, whose wage was twelve, fourteen, sixteen dollars a day. One of Anni's boys, Otto, aged four, was playing outside in the bit of yard. He eyed his aunt coolly, accepted a small sack of hard candies which she presented to him, followed her into the house, which she entered at the rear.

Anni was busy at her housework. Anni was always busy at her housework. Anni was twenty-seven and looked thirty-five. Between the two women no love was lost, but to-day their manner toward each other was indefinably changed. Helmi was no longer the debtor. Helmi was an independent and free woman, earning her twenty a week. Anni was a married woman, bound, tied, harried by a hundred household tasks and trials. The two talked in their native tongue.

"Well, how goes it?"

"Always the same. You are lucky. You have your day off, you can run out and have a good time."

"She wanted me to stay home to-day and go tomorrow instead. I soon showed her and that daughter of hers."

They went into that in detail. Their pale blue eyes were triumphant.

"You are early to-day. Did you eat?"

"No. Coffee only."

"I'll fix you some *kaalikääreitä* left over from the children's lunch."

Helmi cast a glance of suspicion at her suddenly suave sister-in-law, but she pulled a chair up to the kitchen table and ate the savoury stuffed cabbage with a good appetite. She had had no Finnish food for almost two weeks. It was good.

Well, she must be going. Going? Already? Where was she running? Helmi supped up the last of the gravy on her plate and rose. Oh, she had much to do! Well, now you are so independent I suppose you will spend all your money. Yes, and suppose I do? What then? Nothing, only Abel is so close with his money. I wish I had a dollar or two of my own to spend. I need so many things. Helmi gave her three dollars, grudgingly. She would do this again and again during the year. She was wild to be gone. She went into the bedroom to look at the baby; powdered her nose; drank a final and hasty cup of coffee, and was off. Anni watched her go, her eyes hard.

A long, long ride this time back to New York. Grand Central. Change. The East Side subway. She was spewed up with the crowd at One Hundred and Twenty-fifth Street; plunged vigorously into its colourful, cheerful hurly-burly. A hundred noises attracted her. A hundred sights lured her. But she knew what she wanted to do. She made straight for the shop where Lempi Parta had bought her dress. Bulging, glittering plate-glass windows brilliant with blues and pinks and reds and gold. We pay highest prices for Liberty bonds and War Savings Stamps.

Helmi entered. The place was full of girls like herself, with bobbed hair and flat faces and broad shoulders and pale blue eyes. Upper East Side Finland was buying its Easter finery. A woman came forward—an enormous woman with an incredible bust, and a measureless waist, and bead trimming, and carrot-coloured hair. And what can I do for you, miss? Helmi made known her wants. The woman emitted a vocal sound; a squawk.

"Miss S.! Oh, Miss S.! Step this way. . . . The young

lady here wants you should show her something in a Alice-blue crêpe."

You did not pay for it all at once, of course. You paid in part, and they took your name and address and the name of the people you worked for. (Helmi used to be most demanding about the accent over the *a's* in Seppala, but she was no longer.) But they obligingly let you take the whole ravishing outfit: Alice-blue dress; blue coat lined with sand crêpe and trimmed with embroidery and edged with a collar of fur; Alice-blue silk hat; beige silk stockings, very sheer; strapped slippers. She hung the boxes and bundles about herself, somehow, joyously. Miss S. was most gracious.

Into the five-and-ten-cent store. A mass of people surged up and down the aisles. They buffeted and banged Helmi's boxes, but she clung to them rigidly. A handkerchief, edged with blue lace. A small flask of perfume. A pocket comb that cunningly folded up on itself. An exhausting business, this shopping. More tiring than a day's housework. She stopped at an unspeakable counter and ordered and devoured a sandwich of wieners with mustard (10c.) and a glass of root beer (5c.) Thus refreshed, she fought her way out to the street.

It was mid-afternoon. She walked placidly up One Hundred and Twenty-fifth Street, enjoying the sights and sounds. Her strong arms made nothing of their burden. Music blared forth from the open door of a radio shop. She stopped to listen, entranced. Her feet could scarcely resist the rhythm. She wandered on, crossed the street. "Heh! Watch it!" yelled a tough taxi driver, just skimming her toes. He grinned back at her. She glared after him; gained the curb. A slim, slick, dark young fellow leaning limply against the corner cigar store window spoke to her, his cigarette waggling between his lips.

"Watch your step, Swensky."

"Shod op!" retorted Helmi, haughtily.

An open-faced orange drink booth offered peppermint taffy in ten-cent sacks. Helmi bought a sack and popped one of the sticky confections between her strong yellow teeth. A fake auction, conducted by a swarthy and Oriental-looking auctioneer, held her briefly. He was auctioning a leprous and swollen Chinese vase. A dollar! A dollar! Who offers a dollar? All right. Who says fifty cents! Twenty-five! Step inside. Come inside, lady, won't you? Don't stand like that in the door. She knew better than that; was on her way. Yet the vase would have looked lovely in a parlour. Still, she had no parlour.

Her pale eyes grew dreamy. She walked more quickly now. When she approached the Finnish Progressive Society building in One Hundred and Twenty-sixth Street there was the usual line of surprisingly important-looking cars parked outside. That portion of New York's Finnish chauffeurdom which had Thursday afternoon to itself was inside playing pool, eating in the building's restaurant, or boxing or wrestling in the big gymnasium. The most magnificent car of them all was not there. Helmi knew it would not be. Vaino was free on Thursday nights at ten.

Her boxes and bundles in hand, Helmi passed swiftly through the little groups that stood about in the hallway. A flood of Finnish rose to her ears, engulfed her. She drew a long breath. Through the open doorway of the restaurant at the rear. The tables were half filled. Girls eating together. Men, with their hats on, eating together. She ordered a cup of coffee and a plate of Finnish bread—hardtack—*näkki leipä*—with its delicious pungent caraway. This she ate and drank quickly, with a relish. The real joy of the day lay still ahead of her.

Into the hallway again and down a short flight of steps to the basement. Through the pool room, murky with smoke, every table surrounded by pliant, plastic figures intent on the game. The men paid no attention to her, nor she to them. Through the door at the far end of the room. A little office. Down a flight of steps. The steam bath, beloved of every Finn.

All her life Helmi had had her steam bath not only weekly but often two or three times a week. On the farm in Finland the bath-house had been built before the farmhouse itself. You used the bath-house not only for purposes of cleanliness, but for healing, in illness, when depressed. The Finnish woman, in the first throes of childbirth, repaired to the soothing, steam-laden atmosphere of the bath-house. The sick were carried there. In its shelves and on its platforms you lay dreamily for hours, your skin shining and slippery with water. The steam bath was not only an ablution, it was a ceremony, a rite.

On Tuesdays and Thursdays the Finnish Society's steam baths were used only by women. The bath woman, huge, blonde, genial, met her, took her fifty cents, gave her a locker. Helmi opened her precious boxes and hung her finery away, carefully, lovingly. The room was full of naked girls. They were as lacking in self-consciousness as so many babies. They crowded round her—her friend Lempi Parta, and, too, Hilja Karbin, Saara Johnson, Matti Eskolin, Aili Juhola.

"Oh, Helmi! How beautiful! How much did you pay? The boys will dance with you to-night, all right!" they cried in Finnish.

She disrobed swiftly, and stood a moment in the moist warmth of that outer room. Her body was strong and astonishingly graceful, now rid of its cheap and bungling clothes. Her waist tapered slim and flexible below the breadth of the shoulders. She walked well. Now she went into the steam room. The hot breath of the place met her. She lifted her face to it, enchanted. She loved it. The air was thick, heavy with steam from the hot water that dropped endlessly down on to the hot steam pipes below, sending up a misty cloud. From out of this veil a half-dozen indolent heads were lifted from bunks that lined the walls. On each bunk lay an undraped figure.

Helmi sat a moment on the edge of a bunk. "Hello! Hello, Elli! How goes it, Mari? Oo, this is good!"

She reclined upon the bunk, gratefully, yieldingly. Every nerve, every fibre, every muscle of her being relaxed in this moist heat. This stolid Finn servant girl became a graceful plastic figure in repose, a living Greek statue. The mist enveloped her. Her eyes closed. So she lay for fifteen minutes, twenty, a half-hour. Out, then, with Lempi and a half-dozen others, into the cold green waters of the big pool, stopping first for a moment under a shower in the room adjoining the steam bath.

One after another they stood at the pool's edge, graceful, fearless, unaffected. This bath, to them, was a sacred institution. It was an important and necessary part of their lives. They dropped then, swiftly, beautifully, flashingly, into the pool's green depths. They swam like mermaids. They had learned to swim in the icy waters of the Finland lakes. Their voices were high and clear and eager, like the voices of children at play. They were relaxed, gay, happy. "Oo, look! Look at me!" they called to each other in Finnish. "Can you do this?"

Back, dripping, into the steam room again. Another half-hour. The shower again. The pool again. Helmi gave herself over to the luxury of a massage at the expert hands of the masseuse. The strong electric human fingers kneaded her flesh, spanked her smartly, anointed her with oils. She felt blissful, alive, new-born. The Mawson kitchen did not exist. Zhoolie Mawson was a bad dream. Mrs. Mawson did not matter—never had mattered. Vaino. Vaino only.

She was so long in donning the beautiful Alice-blue finery that Lempi and the rest became impatient. But at last it was finished. She surveyed herself radiantly. The flat Finnish face glowed back at her from the mirror. Helmi could never be pretty. But she approached it as nearly now as she ever would.

She would not curl her hair now. That she would do after she had had her supper. She was ravenously hungry.

They would not eat at the building restaurant. They

were tired of it. They would go to Mokki's, on Madison, just off One Hundred and Twenty-fifth. A real Finnish meal. Here they sat at a table for four and talked and laughed in subdued tones, as does your proper Finnish girl. And they ate! Mrs. Mawson would have opened her eyes. They ate first *marja soppa*, which is an incredible soup of cranberries and cornstarch and sugar. They had *mämmi* and cream. They had salt herrings with potatoes. They had *riisi puuro*, which is, after all, little more than rice pudding, but flavoured in the Finnish manner. They drank great scalding cups of coffee. It was superb to see them eat.

It was nearly eight. Helmi must still curl her hair, carefully. This you did in the women's room at the Finnish Society's building. She scanned the line of motors at the curb for the great car—no, it was not there. That was as it should be. The hair-curling business took a half-hour. The room was full of girls changing their shoes; changing their stockings; changing their dresses; combing their hair, curling it; washing.

Helmi and Lempi were going to the play that was given in the theatre two flights up. Another fifty cents. Helmi did not begrudge it. She loved to dance, but she would wait. She would be fresh for ten o'clock. At ten, though the play would not be finished, she would leave for the dance upstairs. She shut her ears determinedly to the music that could faintly be heard when the door opened to admit late-comers. The play was presented by members of the Finnish Society's theatrical group, made up of girls like Helmi and boys like Vaino. Helmi watched it absorbedly. It was, the programme told you in Finnish, *The Second Mrs. Tanqueray*. Helmi and Lempi found it fascinating and true and convincing.

Ten o'clock. They vanished. They deserted Thalia for Terpsichore. They spent another ten minutes before the dressing-room mirrors. The dance hall was crowded. Rows of young men, stolid of face, slim, appraising, stood near the door and grouped at the end of the room partnerless, watching the dancers. Straight as a shot Helmi's eyes found him. How beautiful he was in his blue suit and his shiny tan shoes! His hair shone like his shoes. His cold blue eyes met hers. Her expression did not change. His expression did not change. Yet she knew he had marked her blue dress, and her sheer silk stockings, and her new strapped slippers.

Wordlessly, she and Lempi began to dance together. Lempi took the man's part. She was very strong and expert. She whirled Helmi around and around in the waltz so that her Alice-blue skirt billowed out, and one saw her straight, sturdy, slim legs to the knees. Her skirt swished against the line of stolid-faced boys as she whirled past; swished against Vaino's dear blue-serge legs. She did not look at him, yet she saw his every feature. He did not look at her. He saw the dress, the stockings, the slippers, the knees. True Finns.

The waltz was over. Soberly and decorously Helmi and Lempi sought chairs against the wall. They conversed in low tones. Helmi did not look at him. Five minutes. The band struck up again. The German polka. He stood there a moment. All about were stolid young men advancing stolidly in search of their equally stolid partners. Helmi's heart sank. She looked away. He came toward her. She looked away. He stood before her. He looked at her. She rose. Wordlessly his great hand clasped her waist. Wordlessly they danced. *One*, two, three, and a *one*, two, three, and *turn*, and *turn*, and *turn*, and *turn*. She danced very well. His expression did not change. Her expression did not change. She was perfectly, blissfully happy.

At twelve it was over. At twelve-fifteen she had deposited her boxes and bundles—the everyday clothes of Cinderella—in the back of the huge proud car that had an engine like a locomotive. She was seated in the great proud car beside Vaino. She was driven home. She was properly kissed. She would see him Thursday. Not Thursday, but *Thursday*. He understood. Every other Thursday.

The day was over. She let herself into the Mawson apartment, almost (but not quite) noiselessly. Mrs. Mawson, sharp-eared, heard her. Zhoolie, herself just returned and not so unhappy as she had been sixteen hours earlier, but still resentful, heard her. Helmi entered her own untidy little room, quickly shut the window which Mrs. Mawson had opened, took off the Alice-blue dress, kicked off the tight new strapped slippers, peeled the silk stockings (a hole in each toe), flung her underwear to the winds, dived into the coarse cotton nightgown and tumbled into her lumpy bed with a weary, satisfied, rapturous grunt.

Zhoolie, in her green enamel bed, thought bitterly: "Stupid lump! Went and sat at her sister's, or whatever it is, all day, swigging coffee. It isn't as if she had had anything to do, really. She didn't do a thing. Not a thing! And I've given her I don't know how many pairs of my old silk stockings."

Mrs. Mawson, in her walnut bed, thought, "They're all alike."

Mr. James G. Mawson slept.

CLASSIFIED

CLASSIFIED

Edna Ferber

CLASSIFIED

TO SEE Miss Bobby Comet emerge each week-day morning from that sunless black hole which was her bedroom was to behold each day a miracle performed. Compared with it the trifling business of the butterfly and the chrysalis was humdrum. It seemed incredible that any human process could have produced from this dim cavern a creature so blonde, so slim, so marcelled, so perfumed. Yet eight-thirty each morning, six mornings in the week, saw the magic achievement. So palpably the work of overnight fairies, you were not surprised to learn that this elfin being regarded food with repugnance.

"I don't want any breakfast, Ma. I'm late as it is."

From Mrs. Henry Comet: "Now you swallow a hot cup of coffee, late or no late. Come home at night and there's no living in the house with you, and no wonder. Not a thing on your stomach all day."

"Eat lunch, don't I?"

"Lunch! Ice-cream soda and a hunk of Danish pastry, if you call that lunch. Lookit how your skin looks! Old as I am I wouldn't insult my insides by any such stuff, day in, day out——"

"Oh, all right, all right! Bring on your cup of coffee, then. I never heard that was so good for the complexion

... Ugh! Lookit that kid stuffing soft boiled egg into her. Makes me sick."

That kid (being Miss Jeannette Comet, aged nine, known in the Comet household as Din, a corruption springing from her own infantile inability to pronounce her given name) regarded her fastidious elder sister with wide eyes over the upturned rim of her milk cup. She put down the cup to retort with scorn as scathing as the decoration of her egg-and-milk-rimmed mouth would permit. "Is that so! Then don't look at me, then, Miss Smarty." Perhaps it should be added that Jeannette's name, with its double consonants and its final vowel, represented Mrs. Henry Comet's last frantic clutch at romance.

To this Miss Bobby Comet, sipping her coffee with wry face, paid only elegant indifference. The very crook of her little finger, aloof as she held her coffee cup, registered contempt. Elegant aloofness was the keynote of Miss Bobby Comet's manner. Yet, five minutes later, on her way to work, as she descended the outer steps of her home (a walkup flat) in West Sixty-sixth Street, New York, you saw with certainty that, elegant and aloof as her manner might be, Miss Bobby Comet herself was only an imitation of the Real Thing. A flawless imitation, a perfect imitation—but an imitation.

How, seeing her, you knew this, it is difficult to say. If, by some feat of ocular gymnastics, regarding her with one eye, you could, at the same moment, have turned the other eye on any young lady of about Miss Bobby's age and manner emerging from her home in, say, East Sixty-sixth Street, New York, you might have been hard put to have discovered just wherein the difference lay. Understand that East Sixty-sixth Street is an address. West Sixty-sixth Street is merely a street. Between the two, east and west, lies only that narrow green oasis known as Central Park. It might as well be a continent. Yet West Sixty-sixth is never more than ten minutes late in adopting the style, dress, and manner of East Sixty-sixth.

So you saw Miss Bobby Comet on her way to work garbed as was the whole modish feminine world of the moment. Smart slim dark tailleur (ready-made, hers); beige silk stockings so sheer as to seem no stockings at all; gay vivid scarf; mannish blouse; tiny cloche hat pulled well down over her ears. A uniform. Every two weeks she had her hair shingled by Emile, of the Plaza. It cost her one dollar and a tip. Every week she had it marcelled. She did not begrudge the money. Regularly she earned twenty-five dollars a week—sometimes thirty, frequently thirty-five, what with the system of commissions and prizes used by the manager of her office. Miss Comet was employed in the Classified Telephoned Want Ad department of a New York morning newspaper. She always spent the twenty-five or thirty, or thirty-five down to the ultimate cent. Usually she was in debt for a fur coat, a crêpe dress, a too-smart hat.

From her wage she contributed four dollars a week to the family budget; generally was late with it and always had to be asked for it. Sometimes—but rarely—she brought home a blouse, a pair of silk stockings, some bit of finery for her mother, or a toy for Din. These she would present carelessly, almost roughly. "Here, I'm sick of seeing you going around with those old socks of mine, full of runs." There was something shamefaced in her giving, as in their receiving. It was their fear of displaying fondness—emotion.

Forty-nine girls, besides Bobby Comet, were employed in the big bright want-ad room. And they, too, were imitations. Their presence, and hers, in a business office, was one of the most absurd and paradoxical sights to be seen in a fantastic and ridiculous age. Their clothes, their faces, their voices, their bodies, their very postures were amusingly incongruous viewed in these surroundings made up of telephones, desks, pads, pencils, files, blackboards, racks.

Up one aisle and down the other the manager walked like an overseer eyeing his slaves. Yet there was nothing of serfdom in their manner or glances toward him. They were capable, independent, industrious. They knew their business. Now and then, in a dull moment, they tossed each other a word of conversation. It was always reminiscent of the night before, and bristling with the masculine pronoun, third person, singular. Their talk in the wash room at the noon hour would have made the occupants of a west-bound Pullman smoker turn pale.

To present Miss Comet, sketchily, would be to present the other forty-nine, or nearly. She was twenty; not too pretty; wise, hard, knowledgeable, slim, cool, disdainful; a lovely painted mouth; eyes that stopped you dead at the entrance, though the sign on them read Come In. Imitation pearls round her throat;

a heavy scent of Ambre Antique at eight dollars the ounce; telephone receiver at ear, pencil in hand, pad on desk, lips close to mouthpiece.

The room buzzed and hummed and crackled with talk. The girls' voices were for the most part, rackingly nasal. They articulated with such care as to render their syllables almost grotesque:

"Astorierr Thur-rrrrreee—uh—levun."

"Well, can you lemme talk to the owner of the gasoline station?"

"No, madam, I am not trying to tell you——"

"Thirty-fi'cents a line——"

"Well, I'm sawry you didn't get any satisfaction. Don't you want to——"

"If you have a vacancy again——"

". . . the largest circulation of any newspaper in New York——"

"I said Astorierr Thuh-rrrrreee-uh—levun!"

In the year and a half during which she had been employed in the Classified Want Ads Bobby Comet had cultivated a soft, lilting, honeyed tone, yet businesslike, withal. It was one of her most valuable trade assets. "Prospects," hearing it, rarely slammed up the receiver in the middle of one of Bobby's sugared speeches. That voice, and a certain soft insistence, added up the extra ten a week in commissions and prizes for her. True, she uttered the same cockney New Yorkese to which the other girls gave speech. They all said verse for voice, and earl for oil, and woild for world, and burled for boiled; when they spoke of ersters they meant the succulent bivalve; and the winged creatures in the park trees were boids to them. It was a trick of speech characteristic of Bobby's class and type, born and reared in New York. If you had charged her with this linguistic peculiarity she would have uttered emphatic denial of its possession.

"My verse! What's the matter with it? I don't pronounce my woids different from any other goil. You got a noive!"

There was something likable about Bobby Comet's hardness. Perhaps it was the amiable frankness with which she confessed it. For the code of Bobby's life might be summed up in the six words with which she commented on her mother's existence, and condemned it. "They'll never get *me* that way." This as she saw her mother at her duties about the five-room flat—daily duties in endless repetition: dish-washing, mopping, cooking, sewing. Tied to the house by a hundred dull tasks. To Bobby her mother represented the thing against which she was fighting—the fate to which she told herself (though not in just these words) she would never submit. Lower middle-class drabness; child-bearing, penny-counting.

Not that Mrs. Henry Comet was a drudge. Not she! True, she was a morning slattern, careless as to hair and apron and shoes. But in the afternoon you were likely to see her blossom in Sixty-sixth Street, on her way to the "L" station and her shopping, in the gayer shades of beaded crêpe, and in a taffeta hat and strapped pumps and beige stockings (discarded as too faded by her daughter).

There was nothing pathetic about Mrs. Henry Comet,

seen from the surface. A plump woman, nearing fifty and looking less than her age.

Between the two—mother and daughter—existed, unknown to either of them, a certain enmity. Neither would have recognized or acknowledged it. But to Bobby this middle-aged unlovely woman represented the thing she must not become. And to the middle-aged unlovely woman Bobby was the creature she would never again be. So when Bobby said, almost venomously, "Believe me, they'll never get *me* that way," there sprang up in Mrs. Comet a resentment mingled with a protective maternal fear for what was inevitably in store for this cool, remote, disdainful young thing with her slim ankles and her bobbed hair and her assurance and her cruelty and her soft red lips, like a puppy's.

"Yeh, I've heard that smart talk before. You'll wake up some day, young lady, and find you've gone and made a swell mess of it."

"Like hell I will," retorted Miss Bobby Comet, elegantly. "I'm no sleep walker."

There was another phrase of which Miss Bobby Comet was fond: "I can take care of myself." Simple enough sounding. To the uninitiated the words might even smack of a sturdy self-reliance. But beneath them was much that was sinister. I can take care of myself. A murky saying, as this girl uttered it, and one that went fathoms deeper than its mere surface meaning would suggest.

To comprehend its full significance one should be allowed at least a glimpse of Miss Bobby Comet between the ages of eighteen months and eighteen years. At eighteen months she had been known as Barbara, a name she later regarded as lacking in chic, and for which she had substituted the briefer and more dashing nickname. When Bobby was Barbara, and eighteen months old, she had begun to take care of herself. At that time the Comets had lived on the fifth floor of a six-story walkup in West Sixty-ninth Street. Their present abode in West Sixty-sixth was one of elegance and affluence compared to that.

The Sixty-ninth Street flat had been two blocks farther west, which put it definitely in an unsavoury neighbourhood swarming with dark-skinned foreigners, slatternly women, bedraggled and unkempt children. Sidewalks and roadway crawled with these latter. There were two small Comet children older than the infant Barbara—Bess, aged four; Martin, three. Din had put in her tardy appearance almost ten years later. The dingy flat building cowered in the very shadow of the great menacing gas tower that reared its huge bulk at the foot of the sordid street so near the river.

Mrs. Comet had no time to take the infant out for an airing in the ramshackle old perambulator that had already done double duty. So Barbara, in her buggy, had been placed in front of the house at the foot of the short flight of dirty steps that led to the sidewalk. The boys of the district swarmed the street, playing baseball and handball in the middle of the road, roller-skating, smoking, committing all manner of devilment. Baseballs and handballs whizzed around the infant's defenseless head. Her eyes grew quick and wary. She developed a genius for dodging an oncoming ball as a seasoned soldier senses the approach of a shell.

In this environment, too, she learned to talk surprisingly early. Before she was two she had a fluent if somewhat unintelligible vocabulary which, if anyone had been able to translate it, would have been found to be made up of odds and ends of gutter jargon; the language of baseball and the street; gossip between slatternly women in kimonos and run-down slippers whose high heels proclaimed them declassed finery. At moments the small Barbara would sit up in her baby carriage with its soiled pillows and its grimy blanket, and hurl invective at the street urchins in baby talk, her absurd rosebud of a mouth uttering obscenities in cheerful unconcern.

Such had been the early environment of Bobby Comet, and of Bess, her older sister now married, and of Mart, her brother. By the time of Din's belated arrival the Comets had moved by slow degrees from the west side near the river to the west side near the Park. The West Sixty-sixth Street flat in which they now lived represented a climax in decent comfort. That is, for Henry Comet and Mrs. Comet. Bobby designated it as a dump. The rental paid was seventy dollars a month. Henry Comet, foreman in a hatband factory, earned twenty-eight hundred a year. Mart, the son, who now at twenty-three earned more than his father at fifty-four, paid his weekly board and made no comment, being a silent and somewhat sinister young man who went his own mysterious way. Bess, now married and herself the mother of two, lived in New Jersey. In Bobby's eyes her married sister represented the very likeness of failure.

Bess had liked pretty clothes, had owned them before her marriage. Yet now she regarded Bobby's finery with a sort of wonder, as though she had forgotten that money could freely be spent for such things. Strangely enough, there was little of envy in her face and voice as Bobby flaunted before the older sister some wisp of georgette or satin; a new hat; an absurd pair of slippers. "My!" she would say, just a shade of wistfulness tingeing her tone, "I'll bet that took a bite out of your pay, all right." Sometimes Bobby, in a burst of generosity, moved by she knew not what in the sight of this harried, dishevelled woman who had been her pretty careless sister of a few years ago, would thrust some piece of finery into her hand. "Here. Take this. It don't look very good on me, anyway. I liked it when I bought it but—I don't know."

"Me? Where'd I wear it? Cooking?"

"Lookit her!" Miss Bobby Comet would say scornfully to her mother after one of Bess's rare and hurried visits to the parental flat. "Two squalling kids and another about due and not twenty-seven yet. And did you see that dress! I don't see how she can let herself go like that."

An expression saddened Mrs. Comet's plump face. "She did look pretty fierce, poor kid. She used to be so dressy, too, Bess did. Wasn't a girl in the block could touch her for style time we lived over in Sixty-ninth. I don't know—I suppose——"

Bobby's mouth drew itself into a hard line. "No sense in letting herself go like that just because she's married. Fred earns good money. She looked a sketch."

At which Mrs. Comet right-about-faced in quick defense of her first-born. "Is that so! Lookit the way she's bringing up those kids. Her money goes into good spinach and meat broth for them instead of everything on her back. You have a flat to take care of and two young ones and you'd soon see how much time you'd have for style."

"Me? Not a chance, lady. They'll never get *me* that way."

"Going to marry a millionaire, I suppose, soon's you get time."

"I might, at that."

"I heard they're tearing each other's coats off trying to get beauties like you to take 'em."

"Yeh? Well, marriage isn't everything, you know."

A steely look narrowed Mrs. Comet's still fine eyes. "Looka here, young lady. Don't you go trying to pull any of that smart stuff or I'll have your father give you the whaling of your life, old as you are, and don't you forget it. And Mart'll have something to say, too. I don't want no Tiernan talk around this flat, and just get that into your head, will you—if there's any room in it for anything besides clothes and paint and powder and dates."

By Tiernan talk Mrs. Comet referred to the widow, Mrs. Tiernan, who lived in the flat next door. Her daughter came to see her briefly every week or two. A strangely luxurious figure she made as she flashed into this block of cheap flats, laundries, bootblack establishments, garages, riding stables, delicatessens, basement groceries. The girl came in a great dark silent motor car which, with its chauffeur, she invariably left at the corner. From heels to chin she was swathed in rich dark mink. Cut-steel buckles glittered at her insteps. A tiny beady-eyed dog poked its quivering nose just outside the furred curve of her elbow. Even Bobby could never hope successfully to imitate such apparel as this one wore.

"She sure married something elegant," Mrs. Tiernan would explain after these visits. "He's a big bug in Wall Street and makes money hand over fist and gives her anything she lays an eye on before she can as much as name it. Married grand, my Ellen—Eleanore."

To this statement Mrs. Comet did not even pay the doubtful compliment of contemptuous reply. She could even feel a little sorry for the widow Tiernan. "Married my foot," she remarked, merely.

There was about the widow Tiernan's mouth a loose look which accounted largely, perhaps, for Ellen—Eleanore's befurred state. No such look marred the forthright features of Mrs. Henry Comet. Which was, doubtless, one reason why Bobby went minkless. Not that Miss Bobby Comet was a Puritan miss. She, perhaps, knew exactly what she meant when she said, "I can take care of myself." Certainly Mrs. Comet and Henry Comet knew little enough of the girl's life outside the five-room flat. For that matter, their son Mart's social life was pretty much a blank to them as well. There they were, the five of them, in a five-room flat. Parlour, front bedroom, back bedroom, dining room, kitchen. Mart slept on a bed couch in the parlour. Mr. and Mrs. Comet occupied the front bedroom. Bobby and Din shared the little dark bedroom with its single window that stared blindly out at the brick wall of an airless court.

It was incredible that a family living in such almost indecent proximity—dwelling in such physical intimacy —should still be able to lead lives so remote and detached from each other. Each had a separate and secret existence into which the others did not penetrate. Even Din, the elfin late-born, had hers. Din was a quiet, almost wistful child given to startlingly frank statements. She could play by herself for hours, pale, self-contained, a trifle malicious. Sometimes Bobby thought she hated her. Sometimes she had for her a feeling of protective tenderness that surprised her.

Take Mart. In some way, at manual training school and at night work in a technical school, Mart had picked up a knowledge of the electrician's craft. A few years at a decent technical college might have made him a trained and competent electrical engineer. But the Comets had had neither the money nor the imagination for that. The boy was skilled, uncommunicative, some-what sinister, very male. His social life he lived quite outside the family circle. Between him and Bobby there existed a sort of fond feud.

They addressed each other mainly in terms of contumely.

"What you made up to represent?" would be his comment, perhaps, on Bobby's toilette for the evening.

Any display of emotion he considered effeminate. For that matter, there was little or no demonstration of affection in the Comet family. The children had never seen a fond look or gesture between the parents. Mrs. Comet now met with rebuff when she attempted to take the long-legged Din into her arms. A caress between Bobby and Mart was undreamed of. Yet for one another the two had a certain hard and astringent feeling of affection.

Mart ate at home, slept there, sometimes condescended to a game of ball after supper in the street before the house with certain hard slim young men of the neighbourhood, like himself dexterous, swift, silent. He never took Bobby out. It never occurred to either of them that he should. Mart had a quick catlike tread, a good deal like an Indian's. He was a marvellous dancer. His telephone communications were mysterious. His outgoing calls were not transacted on the home instrument. These he consummated for the most part at the corner cigar store at Sixty-sixth and Columbus. You saw him leaning indolently against the glass door of the booth, a cigarette waggling expertly in his lips.

But he had frequent incoming calls. Mrs. Comet was sometimes exasperated by the young ladies who called up, and sometimes sorry for them. "Is Mr. Comet in? I'd like to speak to him . . . Oh, isn't he? Are you expecting him? . . . No . . . No, I'll call again."

When they asked for Mr. Comet she knew well that these high nasal voices were not craving the boon of conversation with the sparse, dry, caustic figure that was Comet père. They wanted Mart. Theirs was little enough satisfaction when they got him. Mart's telephonic conversation was as tight and terse as Mart himself. It seemed to consist almost entirely of brief negatives.

One could just catch the plaintive interrogation of the feminine voice at the other end of the wire. Always the rising inflection. The pleading note. It was met by Mart's firm negation:

"No, I can't to-night . . . No, I'm pretty busy this week . . . No, you better not . . . I'll give you a ring, maybe, later'n the week . . . No, I tell you I ain't . . . Well, I can't help that . . . No, I might go outa town Sunday . . . Huh? . . . No."

Sometimes there was wrung from Ma Comet, out of sheer sympathy for the unseen feminine pleaders, an objection in behalf of her sex.

"Mart Comet, I don't see how you can talk so stinkin' to those girls over the 'phone. I've a good notion to tell 'em, next time they call you, that they're fools to waste their time over a bum like you."

"Wisht you would."

"Time I was a girl they didn't go chasing the fellas like that. Telephoning all the time, the silly things."

"Time you were a girl you never heard of a telephone."

"Well, and if we had of, Mr. Smarty, we wouldn't of used it crying and slopping over no fella—least of all no fella like you."

Yet she admired this son of hers, and loved him, and was secretly gratified at his indifference to feminine wiles. She knew that he would marry some day suddenly and without preliminary announcement. She dreaded that day, yet longed for it; never spoke of it. Mart was never home in the evening. None of the family knew where he went.

Miss Bobby Comet, too, mysteriously disappeared almost every evening. She rarely was called for, though sometimes a yellow taxi waited, panting, for her in the street. Its occupant, having rung the bell marked Comet, did not come up. It was unbelievable that Mrs. Comet, lower middle-class American mother, thus allowed her daughter nightly to fare forth. That she should do so was typical of her class.

Bobby, like Mart, ate and slept at home. But unlike him, she sometimes stayed home evenings. On these evenings she was given to washing her hair, manicuring, doing odds and ends of sewing and refurbishing of finery, performing mysterious rites before the mirror. Often, as her older sister was dressing for the evening, Din would stand in the doorway or perch on the bed, watching her as she made up her face in the pattern of the day —cream, well rubbed in; powder; an expert application of mandarin rouge high up on the cheek bones and near the temples; then a dusting of powder again. A scarlet cupid's bow painted on her lips, deceiving no one, and not meant to. A black line marking the plucked eyebrows. Nail rouge and buffer. Powder on her throat. A generous spray of perfume on hair and arms. A dab of it just behind the ears and just above the upper lip, for preparedness. Din's eyes were round and owlish in the little face that was losing its baby contours and emerging into adolescence. She was mathematically aware of every pair of silk stockings possessed by Bobby. Her information regarding Bobby's pink silk underwear, her bottles of perfume, toilette water, cold cream; her mysterious and somewhat grubby array of scissors, burnishers, and various red stuffs with which she was forever smearing lips, cheeks, and nails, was complete.

To Bobby's surprise and annoyance she had said gravely, one evening, after regarding in silence her elder sister in the complicated art of making up:

"When I grow up I'm not going to put stuff like that on my face all the time."

"Oh, aren't you, Miss Nosey! And why not?"

Din looked at her sister, straight. She shrugged her thin little shoulders with a startlingly grown-up air. "Oh, I won't. Not by the time I'm grown up. I'll be different from you."

Suddenly then Bobby Comet saw herself ten years hence, old, done for, out of it, the bloom gone. Din would be twenty, fresh, different. Different from her. Already she was learning different things at school, wearing clothes unlike those of Bobby's childhood.

Dressed, Bobby emerged with an unwonted dash of genuine scarlet flaming oddly beneath the artificial colouring on her cheeks. She addressed her mother seated in the parlour window overlooking the street.

"Pity a person can't even dress in this house without having that brat nosing around. Sitting right on top of you. No more privacy in this joint than in the street."

Mrs. Comet turned from the window to eye her irate and dressy daughter. "Are they wearing 'em as short as that again, for He'm sake! . . . And what's eating you now? What's she done? What you done, Din? Tell Mama."

"Nothing," replied Din gravely. "I didn't do a single solitary thing."

"Tell Mama! Tell Mama!" mimicked Bobby, in a cold fury. "She's the one that counts. It's always Din, Din! Look at the shoes you buy for her and what you used to buy for me when I was a kid. Anything was good enough for me. Now she's got to have the toes just so and the heels just right, and everything. She won't have corns like me when she's my age. Look at what she gets to eat, and what I got! She's got to have her chops and her spinach. And at school! French! And special this and special that, and all this new hygiene stuff. You learned on me and Bess, all right. We sure got the worst of it."

Mrs. Comet met this outburst mildly. "Done the best I could for you with what I had to do with. Your pa never was a big earner."

"Oh, I don't know." This from Henry Comet emerging from behind his evening paper. "I guess I've always provided as good as the next one. Good enough for me, anyway, if it isn't for your tony daughter."

"This dump!" In contempt, from Bobby, on the wing.

"If I could of had this, time I was married, I'd thought I was in paradise," began Mrs. Comet, in reminiscent mood. "Two rooms is what we had, over on Tenth Street, and had to go to the hall for every drop of water. And thought I was lucky to have that and maybe you will, too, some day if you're not——"

But Bobby Comet had flung out of the house.

Mrs. Comet returned to her window. Henry Comet went back to his paper. Din pursued some quiet game of her own. Sometimes you saw Henry Comet, silent, sparse, dried-up, regarding this family of his over the top of his paper. And his eyes were the eyes of a stranger looking upon strangers. Henry Comet had come of a good old Vermont family of the codfish type. Perhaps he, too, had his secret thoughts as he squinted up through his cigar smoke. Sometimes Mr. and Mrs. Comet and Din went to the movies in the evening. Frequently Henry Comet went alone. He liked romantic pictures, with deeds of dash and daring in them.

Such was the Comet family life. Theirs was the spendthrift and almost luxurious existence of the American working class. Ready-made clothes; white shoes; Sunday papers; telephone; phonograph; a radio; pork roast; ice-cream; the movies. A somewhat sordid household, certainly, but comfortable, too. Bookless, of course. Extravagant with its quarters, its half dollars, and its dollars.

If Miss Bobby Comet had been less imitative and less adaptable she might have been more content. But all about her, in a luxurious city, she saw luxury. Seeing it, she craved it. Craving it, she reached out for it and got, now and then, a handful. Being fundamentally a pretty decent girl, and further sustained by the fairly solid background of the Comet household, she worked hard, earned her money, spent it selfishly, took what was offered, and gave no thought of to-morrow.

For the most part she went about with married men. She drove with them in taxis. You saw her and other girls of her type dining in famed restaurants and hotels along Broadway, Fifth Avenue, and the Forties. She dressed well and in excellent taste. She ate prettily and fastidiously. She had her cigarette with her coffee. She had learned to eye the rose-shaded room with a look of cool indifference. She had caught the trick of ordering one dish, and that very special and expensive. She had learned to say, "Tell the waiter I want lemon, not vinegar, in my French dressing." She was an excellent imitation.

Her escorts were, as a rule, dull and somewhat paunchy gentlemen grown weary in the pursuit of business. Her youth attracted them, and her commonplace prettiness, her flippant tongue, her audacity, her superciliousness. She possessed, too, a certain bubbling quality most refreshing to these doggishly inclined gallants, approaching middle age and secretly weary of the connubial kimono and the humdrum of *Geschäft*. Bobby Comet took what these offered and gave little in return. She was alert, greedy, calculating, frank. There was nothing pathetic about Bobby's position with regard to these gentlemen. They were the victims. She the despoiler. If they protested she left them. There were always others. When she had been younger— sixteen or seventeen—she had gone about with boys of her own class. She had frequented the public dance hall at the height of the craze, where she and her boy had performed with incredible expertness the intricate mechanical steps of the day, their bodies locked in a strangely sexless embrace. She almost never now went about with such as these.

During working hours she and the other girls discussed their social triumphs with a frankness and un-

concern that would have appalled their victims of the
preceding night.

"Any good?"

"Oh, yeh. Dinner at the Royale."

"Show?"

"Yeh. Music Box."

"Again!"

"My third time. But I've seen everything else. I
didn't stick through the whole show, though, I told him
I had to get home and grab my beauty sleep. Was he
sore!"

But not so much of this as to interfere with the work
of the day. Bobby rather enjoyed her work. It had in it
the elements of change and of uncertainty. Unseen
faces at the other end of the wire. Unknown voices.
Rebuff or success—one never knew which might be encountered. Certain regulars came to know her over the
telephone, and she them; boarding-house keepers;
landladies of rooming-houses. At home she would occasionally comment on them, caustically.

"The same rooms that were warm and cosy last winter are cool and airy, now it's July. I could die at 'em."

Bobby, expert in her calling, no longer took incoming
unsolicited ads. It was her duty to search out possible
advertisers, many of whom had placed their want ads
in the classified columns of rival papers. Others had
advertised unsuccessfully once or twice, perhaps, in
the columns of her own sheet. These last she urged to
insert their ad for a full week, at a decreased weekly
rate.

Bobby was very good at this. Her voice was sympathetic, clear, firm. She had had two years of high school, and a business school course. Her English, when she pleased, was grammatical enough, though at home she spoke the slovenly speech of the household. She rarely met with failure, hence her increased weekly wage. A seven-day ad meant a fat commission. A set of them meant a prize plus the commission. Bobby Comet used a form; a code. Lips close to the telephone mouthpiece she got her number; waited; then:

"This is Miss Comet talking . . . Miss Comet . . . Yes . . . I want to talk to the proprietor of the garage, please . . . No, I want to talk to him personally . . . Tell him Miss Comet wants to talk with him." Another wait. Always just a tinge of trepidation, which added zest to the game.

Then: "Is this the proprietor of the garage? I want to know if you have succeeded in selling your garage. You advertised it for sale, didn't you? . . . Have you sold it? . . . No, I don't want to buy it. I want to help you sell it . . ."

More talk. Arguments. A strong friendly note in the voice. Nothing offensive. Her voice encouraging, not too insistent, but firm. It was surprising to see how often she won them over. But it was hard work, too, and a good deal of a strain, this throwing one's personality into the telephone and trying to make it penetrate the other end of the wire.

Sometimes an irate housewife, called to the telephone and sensing a possible bridge invitation or a bit of gossip, slammed up the receiver on hearing Bobby's dulcet statement or request. But Bobby was undismayed by this. Failure to-day might mean success to-morrow.

"Mr. Meyer? This is Miss Comet. I see you haven't sold your cottage yet out at Jamaica . . . No, I'm not bothering you—at least I hope I'm not. I'm just interested in seeing you sell that little cottage. I want to help you. Now, why don't you give us a chance? You won't regret it . . ."

It was thus she met Jesse—or, rather, met him again. For as it turned out he had been a fellow student of Mart's at the technical night school and had even come to the house with Mart once, briefly. Bobby had been seventeen then. She did not remember him. Disguised as a mere telephone number he had advertised a storage garage for sale, using the classified columns of a rival morning paper. Immediately Bobby was hot on the trail of the unknown. The usual formula: "This is Miss Comet talking, I want to speak to the owner of the garage . . . Miss Comet . . ."

"This is the owner. Who'd you say? . . . Spell it."

Bobby spelled it, graciously.

"Comet? Say, I used to know a——You got a brother Mart?"

"Why—yes."

Don't you remember? Well, what do you know about that! It's a small world. Yeh. Well, that's funny. They laughed a little, grew friendly at once. His was a clipped way of speaking, very engaging. No, he hadn't got any satisfaction out of that ad in the other paper. No, he didn't want to try her paper. No use throwing good money after bad. They'd soaked him hard enough already. You see, it was like this. He had bought this garage thinking they were going to make a boulevard of this roadway. Yeh, fella he'd bought it from said they were. Showed him the plans, and everything. And they were, too, only they changed their minds. Something about graft, or city hall, or something. Anyway, there he was, stuck with the garage, and maybe five years before they began work on the street. He wanted to get out of it and go back to his regular job, working for somebody else. Let the other fella do the worrying. He'd take less than he'd paid for it, just to get out of it. No, he didn't think he'd advertise.

That ended the conversation for the day. Next day Bobby called him up again. Well, no, he hadn't sold it. We-e-e-ell, yes, he might try it once. A week! Oh, no! Well, four days then. Say, it's that voice of yours, I guess. It's the voice with the smile that wins. Yeh. Say, what'd you say your first name was? Huh? Bobby! Say, that's a h— a funny name for a girl. Bobby said it was no funnier than his name for a man. Well, that's right, too. Guess they'd better swap names. How'd you like to try my name for a change? Jesse Lloyd Whiting. Guess his mother must have read it in a book or something. Call me Jesse. Just Jesse. Ha! That's a good one!

She sold his garage for him, wording the ad herself, craftily. It was he, then, who called her on the telephone. He thanked her. He was jubilant. His old job again. Little old pay envelope looked pretty good to him . . . To-night? No, she had an engagement. To-morrow night? Sawry.

A moment's meaningful silence at his end of the wire. Then his speech more clipped than ever. All right, Miss Comet. Much obliged for your kindness. See you at church some time (a phrase). My regards to old Mart.

He had hung up. Bobby remained staring thoughtfully into the telephone.

That night, at the supper table, she spoke of him to Mart.

"Who? Whitey! Sure I remember him. He was a swell kid. Smart, too, only always getting it in the neck. Invented a kind of a tire lock and somebody swiped it away from him and he never got anything out of it. Say, I'd like to see him some time. Tell him, will you?"

"How'll I tell him?" said Bobby, loftily.

Mart threw her a swift hard glance. "Oh. Yeh. Well. Strictly a business acquaintance, huh? One of these mechanic persons, what? Deah, deah! Listen to me, me wench. Whitey's got it so all over these fat cloak-and-suiters I see you running around with that you wouldn't know how to talk to him if you did have a chance, which I bet you never did have. And don't you forget it."

She called the garage next day. No, he wasn't there any more. This place has changed hands. She might try him at such and such a number. She tried him. No, he was out. Any message? No, she'd call again. Something about this sounded vaguely familiar to her. That was what the girls said who called Mart unsuccessfully.

Anyway, he'd probably telephone her in a day or so. They always did. She waited. He did not call her. Two days passed. Three. Four. A week. Suddenly, in an idle moment one afternoon, she called him again. When she heard his oddly clipped speech at the other end of the wire her heart gave a queer little leap. She gave him Mart's message as an excuse. Then, this time, it was she who said, "To-night?" That little second of silence from his end.

Sorry, but he was working to-night. The silence again, and, oddly, she felt her cheeks burning. Then he said, coolly and without urge, "How about to-morrow night?"

At eight o'clock next night he rang the bell marked Comet. He negotiated the three flights of stairs and the dim hallways, rang the doorbell, came in, and was introduced to the family. Bobby hadn't remembered him as being so good-looking. Well, he wasn't, exactly, but —I don't know. His eyes, wide apart, and ardent. And young! Just a kid. Like Mart.

He was quiet and a little shy, and yet he was self-possessed. He made a little fuss over Mrs. Comet without seeming to. Mart had stayed home to meet him. Bobby thought the two of them would never finish their stupid reminiscing. Had he come to see her or Mart? She tapped a restless toe. She wished she had never started anything. He'd take her to a movie, she supposed, and maybe an ice-cream soda afterward, and think he had had a big night.

He stood up, looked at her inquiringly. "I've got a car downstairs Miss—Bobby. That is, I suppose you could call it a car. It goes on four wheels without pushing. I kind of made it myself out of a couple of tin cans and a piece of wire and an old cigar box or something. It's got parts in it of every car from a Rolls Royce to a

Ford. If you'd like to run up along the river somewhere and have a bite and maybe dance———?"

The evening was warm, velvety, starlit. The mongrel car wasn't so bad-looking, its bar sinister hidden under a smart coating of maroon paint. Bobby Comet felt suddenly young, exhilarated, and very, very pure. Occasionally, as they wound along the river, she sang a bit of a song of the hour. Once she was faulty for a bar or two, at the end of a chorus, and he corrected her, whistling it softly, clearly, and in perfect rhythm.

He did not talk much. He reminded her, somehow, of Mart; and she liked him for that, which should have warned her. But she knew nothing of the theories of the Viennese psychoanalysts. They danced, easily and wordlessly and tirelessly, in the outdoor dancing pavilion of a roadhouse. Bobby loved the feel of his hard muscular flat body. The tired business men were convex where Jesse was concave; and they were, furthermore, what Mr. Mantalini would have called demned moist and unpleasant. Bobby Comet sighed; but blissfully.

"Tired?" Jesse asked her.

"No."

His hard lean arm pressed her close to him. But when she looked up at him his young face was set and stern. Between dances they ate. At the figures on the supper card she hesitated—she who always ordered with such insolent unconcern. He sensed this at once. He grinned engagingly.

" 'S all right. You don't need to be scared. I'm not broke. You take just what you'd order with your— regular friends."

Her regular friends. She looked at him through narrowed lids. "What do you know about my regular friends?"

He glanced at her clothes—her smart clothes that were almost just right. He looked down at his hands which he never could quite free from the grime of his calling. She thought she knew what he was going to say, but he surprised her.

"I could tell by the way you danced."

"Danced!" She rather prided herself on her dancing.

"Yeh. Kind of cautious. As if you'd forgotten how to let go. Dancing with the fat old boys who're short on the breath."

A flame of scarlet scorched her cheeks that hadn't felt such warmth in years.

He did not kiss her on the way home. They talked but little. Yet she felt strangely soothed, rested, serene, and somehow, light. His manipulation of the crazy little car was smooth, expert, flawless. He did not ask to see her again. She waited, looking up at him. She waited.

"Well, good-night. See you at church," he said.

An icy clamp coiled itself around her heart and squeezed it dry. She hesitated. He said nothing.

"Call me up some time."

"Sure," he replied, gravely and politely.

Almost in horror she heard herself saying, "This week?"

And in equal horror his answer—"No. I'm busy this week." Mart's answer.

She turned and went up the steps. He climbed nimbly into the ramshackle little car and was off.

Oh, well, she told herself at the end of the week, what was he, anyway, but a greasy mechanic. A kid. Yet when she came home at six—"Anybody 'phone me?"

"No."

Bobby Comet took to staying home evenings. When the telephone rang she flew to it, beating the impish Din by a scant second. Her voice, as she answered it, was low, vibrant. "Hello! . . . Oh." You would not have believed that a voice could change so in a breath; become flat, lifeless, without timbre. "Hold the wire. I'll call him." Then, to Mart, "One of your janes."

Once Mart said, "Seen Whiting since?"

Her heart gave a great leap. Her face was impassive. "Who?"

"Whiting. Jesse Whiting."

"Oh—him. No. Forgot all about him."

Mart's cold young eyes narrowed shrewdly, speculatively. "Then you're the first girl ever has."

She fought the impulse to ask her question, and lost. "Why? Is he such a heartbreaker?"

"Is he! Why, say! He taught me all I know," said Mart modestly. The obvious answer to that rose to her lips and was spoken by them, lifelessly. She took no pleasure in the retort.

She'd show him. If he ever did call up again she'd show him. Let him ask her to go out with him again and she'd show him.

A week—ten days—two weeks. Then, unexpectedly, when she had quite given him up, his oddly clipped speech at the other end of the wire. And then her own voice, with a deep note in it, saying, "To-night? Why—yes—I'd love to."

"And," said Mrs. Henry Comet, two months later, "what's he earn?"

"Enough," Miss Bobby Comet answered.

"How much?" asked Mrs. Comet again, insistently. Bobby's head came up defiantly. "Forty a week."

"My God!" said Mrs. Comet, piously. "Where you going to live on that! And how?"

A look of triumph came into Bobby's face. "We were looking at places Sunday. There's two rooms at a Hundred and Eighty-sixth Street——"

"Oh, my gosh to goodness!" said Mrs. Comet. Then, suddenly, "Why, that's grand, Bobby. It's kind of far away from us, and all. But it'll be grand, to start on." Suddenly the two women were closer than they ever had been. A something had sprung up between them, binding them together for the moment. Love and pity shone in Mrs. Henry Comet's face, transfiguring it.

"Sure," said Miss Bobby Comet, happily; and looked about the five-room flat in West Sixty-sixth Street. The dump. "Say, we couldn't expect to have a place like this. Not to start with."

HOLIDAY

HOLIDAY

Edna Ferber

HOLIDAY

IT HAD been raining for three days in Newark, New Jersey. Newark is unlovely enough on a gay May morning. After three days of March rain it is sodden beyond bearing. It was the rain as much as anything that caused the Cowans to decide on an Atlantic City holiday. That and Pa Cowan's bronchial cold and Evelyn's everlasting telephoning and Evelyn's children's noise and the general state of irritability and waspishness to which the whole family was reduced after three days of being cooped up. Six—not counting the girl—in a seven-room flat are likely to cut jagged edges in each other's nerves, even if they are a devoted family.

And the Cowans were a devoted family. They spoke of it often. "We're very devoted." They were always saying, "Let me do that," or "I'll go. You sit still," and "Here's a nice juicy piece just looking at you. Don't you want it?" Naturally they quarrelled a good deal. Take, for example, Evelyn's telephoning. It was enough, Carrie said, to drive a stone image crazy. Still, before taking Evelyn's telephoning, it might be well to take the family one by one.

There was Pa Cowan, sixty-nine; Ma, sixty-five; Evelyn, the widowed daughter, thirty-three; Evelyn's two children, Dorothy and Junior, aged four and seven respectively; and Carrie Cowan, the unmarried daughter, aged—Carrie the unmarried daughter. Not that Carrie seemed to mourn her maiden condition; nor was she reticent about her years. She was always the first to speak of these, and jokingly. She was quite comical about her virgin state and said in a roomful of Evelyn's married friends, "If you're going to talk like that I guess a young gal like me had better leave the room."

Evelyn, after her husband's death, had come back home to live. It was pretty hard, she told her old Newark friends, after you've lived in New York for nine years, and had your own lovely things and everything to do with. Of course, she never said this in the presence of the family except sometimes when Carrie was there.

Carrie went about almost exclusively with married people. She made a fourth at bridge or mah jong. She filled a last-minute vacancy at dinner. She had bought and presented dozens of baby jackets, rattles, and teething rings. She heard the intimate talk and the innuendo of the married women in Evelyn's group. She cried gaily, "Not knocking anybody's husband, but I wouldn't change places with any of you." But within her someone else cried out, "Oh, God!"

You saw a woman in the late thirties with a rather swarthy skin like her mother's—Evelyn was fair—and the figure of the unwed woman approaching middle age, rather flat as to bust and ample below the waist. She made a trim appearance though and was able to say with her married women friends: "I know I don't look it. Nobody thinks I weigh within fifteen pounds of that. It's because I carry all my weight right here. No, it doesn't show, thank goodness, but it's almost impossible to take it off."

It wasn't as if Carrie hadn't had her chance. There was a good deal of mystery about it. When she was twenty-nine there had been a man, and an engagement with everything announced, and Pa Cowan was going to take him into his own business. Cotton goods. Then Pa Cowan had made some investigations and the man was no longer seen, and Ma Cowan said that Carrie had had a lucky escape. Strangely enough, it was hard to make Carrie see her luck. Red-eyed and blotchy from weeping she had said over and over, "I don't care. I don't care. I'd have married him anyway."

"Yes," Ma Cowan had retorted, "and been miserable the rest of your life."

"I'm miserable anyway."

"Not half as miserable as you would have been if you'd married him."

"How do you know? Anyway I'd have had——" She stopped there and her face had twisted comically and tragically and her hands had reached out into the empty air clutching futilely after something that was slipping out of her life forever.

Carrie worked in her father's office now four days a week. She was most efficient. At dinner time she talked a good deal about the things that had happened in the cotton-goods business during the day.

"We sent out the city salesman, Goodman, with some swatches and about three o'clock they telephoned and said, 'Look here, I thought you were going to send your city salesman——'"

From Evelyn, "Junior, eat your spinach."

Ma Cowan, "I'd get a black faille crêpe if I had any place to wear it."

"You go out as much as most women your age, Mother."

"Where do I go?"

Pa Cowan, spruce, a little tremulous, brownish splotches on the backs of his hands and at the temples: "Seems nobody stays where they belong any more. Run, run, that's all they do. The world's gone crazy. Florida and Bermuda and I don't know where. Koch was saying to-day you can't get a sailing on a boat for Europe for love or money, and here it's January and the worst sailing on the Atlantic of the whole year."

Pa Cowan, in the cotton-goods business, wanted to go to Florida and Bermuda and he didn't know where. Oh, how he wanted to go sailing on the Atlantic in January! He said to himself, "Here I am sixty-nine, and nothing's ever happened to me." Pa Cowan had always meant to live the life of a Robert Louis Stevenson hero, though he had never read R. L. S. But he had gone into the cotton-goods business at twenty-four and there he still was at sixty-nine. Another writer with whom he was unfamiliar was Mr. Thoreau, so he did not know that the line about most men living lives of quiet desperation was applicable to himself. He dreamed a good deal about ships and the sea; about forests and tigers and mountains and beautiful maidens blonde and slim.

Ma Cowan had always been dark and heavy. In the last ten years the silvering of her hair had relieved the sallowness of her face. She had carried her weight well, but it always had distressed her, too. That which in a girl of twenty-five had been unsightly and disproportionate was now in the woman of sixty-five merely ample, comfortable, and not unfitting. Yet Ma Cowan, all unsuspected—perhaps even by herself—still had visions of herself suddenly transformed into a slim wisp of gold and cream and roses; a lily maid; a wraith all flame and chiffon. This while she knew that her waist even in a stylish stout had never measured less than forty.

The Cowans lived in Tichenor Street, which, to one knowing Newark, definitely placed them. Tichenor Street was old, respectable, middle-class Newark. But like many another old street it was beginning to grow shabby and careless and down at heel. Its respectability was leaning almost imperceptibly toward that unfastidiousness which degenerates into sordidness. Just around the corner you already noted those grisly harbingers of approaching decay—undertakers' parlours, private hospitals, midwives' signs, delicatessens, cheap new flats.

Since her return to the parental roof Evelyn was always urging her family to leave Tichenor Street and take a stucco and tile house in the Forest Park section or on Parker Street, or even out of Newark in one of the Oranges. With that brief taste of New York still sweet in her mouth that now was filled with ashes and wormwood, Evelyn was secretly and fiercely ambitious for social prestige. Pretty, slim, and not without charm, she thought of herself as presiding at small intimate dinners, rose-shaded, delicate, reticent; of queening it at evening affairs, large yet exclusive, at which people did not begin to arrive until ten. She loathed Tichenor Street. She actually humbled herself in order to scrape acquaintance with people who might be of benefit to herself or to the children, Dorothy and Junior, fifteen years hence.

"We've always been a very devoted family," said the Cowans. "We live for each other. . . . I'll go. . . . Don't you bother. . . . Let me do that for you. . . . Can I help you? . . ."

Ma Cowan, Pa Cowan, Evelyn, Carrie—four strangers living together. For all unsuspected:

"Come, Adventure," cried Pa Cowan, "before I die!"

"Come, Beauty," cried Ma Cowan, "before it is too late!"

"Come, Love!" cried Carrie. "I am starving for want of you."

"Come, Power!" cried Evelyn. "I have always dreamed of you."

On coming back to Newark Evelyn had said: "Let me take some of the housekeeping worries off your hands, Mama. I'll do the marketing and things. It's little enough for me to do, goodness knows, after all you and Pa have——" Red-rimmed eyes and a quick handkerchief.

But that hadn't lasted long. Evelyn thought it foolish to walk a block to save two cents on a head of lettuce. Ma Cowan thought it criminal not to. House-cleaning under Evelyn's régime was a fairly painless process, with a scrub woman in to help and a man to do the lifting and climbing. Mrs. Cowan made of the house-cleaning period a St. Bartholomew's Day.

Even in the summer the Cowans stayed pretty close to Tichenor Street. They said that Newark was a regular summer resort, it was so cool, and you could get out to the beaches in a jiffy any time you wanted to. Besides, years of thrift had made them cautious. But this Atlantic City jaunt of three days' duration had come about almost of itself. Rain, cough, snuffles, nerves, the noise of children housed too long, Evelyn's everlasting telephoning.

In the last three days she had, it seemed to Ma Cowan and Carrie, said the same thing over and over a hundred times, seated at the little wobbly black imitation oak telephone table and jotting down meaningless figures and curlicues on the pad of paper as she talked.

"Hello! . . . Yes. . . . Oh, hello, Daisy. Isn't that weird! I was just this minute thinking of you. . . . Oh, I'm fine but the rest of the family's laid low. Colds. I'm keeping Junior home from school because he has a little—(Dorothy, Mother can't hear a word when you pound on the floor like that. Stop it, dear.) . . . He has a little temperature and I thought I'd just . . . What? What did you say? I couldn't catch that last—(Lover, take that out of sister's mouth this minute! You'll kill her.) . . . Aren't they terrible! They're simply fiendish after being cooped up . . . I wanted to get out to see the moire overblouses that Bamberger's adver—(Put that down! Put it *down*, Mother said! Put it . . .)" Crash! Wails. Tears.

Ma and Carrie had a conference in Ma Cowan's bedroom. "If I have to stand much more of this I'll be a raving, tearing maniac, that's all."

It was decided suddenly that Ma and Pa Cowan were to go away. Atlantic City. The ocean air would do them good. Out of doors all day. One of the girls would go with them. Evelyn, you go. No, you. It'll do you good. You need it more than I. No, I won't leave the children. You're with them too much, that's the trouble. The trouble with whom, please? Oh, nobody.

In the end Carrie went. The three took the eleven o'clock morning train. It was called the Atlantic City Special. Suddenly the sun had come out warm and golden after the three dour days. On Evelyn's face, as she stood in the doorway of the Tichenor Street house waving them good-bye in the spring sunshine, there was a look of anticipation and of release. Carrie saw plans maturing secretly in Evelyn's eyes. Carrie thought: "I'll bet she's going to give a party while we're gone. The girls in for luncheon—or maybe even a dinner with the husbands too, and that bachelor brother-in-law of Daisy's. And her own silver and china and linen unpacked for it."

They bumbled away in the yellow taxi toward the station and Atlantic City. Evelyn went into the house and shut the door and began to telephone. Junior and Dorothy were drawing with coloured crayons. "My angels," said Evelyn. "Mother's angels. It's brightening up. You can both go out just as soon as it gets a little dryer. Hello! . . . Daisy? . . . Listen. The family's gone to Atlantic City . . ."

The Atlantic City Special was filled with holiday seekers. Plump ladies in black crêpe and sly diamond brooches pinned on one shoulder to no purpose. Sleek gentlemen in spats, and yellow gloves which they did not remove, and a great many early afternoon editions of the New York papers. Pa had brought along the Newark *News*. Carrie wished he'd stop reading it, all spread out like that. The sleek gentlemen ordered bubbling water in green bottles from the buffet car because ordering charged water from the buffet car was the thing to do on the Atlantic City Special.

Pa Cowan, on a holiday, was no niggard. Seats in the parlour car. No stopping at one of the picayune ramshackle side-street hotels but at a great fantastic rococo pile on the Boardwalk itself. The doorman and elevator attendants wore uniforms of French blue with scarlet lapels and pipings and facings and gold buttons and white gloves. Their splendour would have made a French general on dress parade appear sombre. They rather overawed Mr. and Mrs. Cowan, but they stimulated Carrie. Their backs were so flat and their waists so tapering and their buttons and gold braid glittered so delightfully.

Two bedrooms, connecting, with a bath for each, and you could see the ocean from both of them. There was cretonne. There were dressing-table lamps with pert little silken shades and a queer ventilator over the door and electric push buttons labelled *Maid*, *Waiter*, *Valet*. A little rush of exhilaration shook the three as they unpacked. The women called between rooms.

"I'm not going to take out anything except just what I need."

"Do you want to have lunch here or somewhere down the Boardwalk?"

From Pa Cowan: "Well, I think you ought to stop fussing over those valises and get out. That's what we came for. I'll meet you downstairs right out in front there. And don't be all day."

Pa was quite masterful when he took his womenfolk on a holiday. A false courage buoyed him. He was conscious of a little feeling of lawlessness within himself, as were the two women. Ruled as they were by each other, bound by a thousand clutching fingers of family devotion, each longed to be free for a brief moment; to fare forth; to prance; to seek the unaccustomed and forbidden.

As they started down the Boardwalk in the seaside sunshine of brilliant noonday you saw a family of three. father, mother, daughter—middle-class, respectable, well-to-do.

"This is great!" said Pa Cowan. "This salt air. Makes you want to step out. Come on, you girls. Step out!" He himself stepped out with what he fancied to be a jaunty athletic stride, his shoulders held stiffly back, his head up. You saw merely an old man, rather rheumy-eyed from the salt tang, jerking along with a stiff and springhalt motion that was at once comic and pathetic. Every now and then he said, "Ha!" and breathed deeply. "Ha!" He thumped his chest. "My cold's better already. I can feel it breaking up."

They walked. They rode in wheel chairs pushed by a chair slave bent double with the load of the three of them. The women stopped and twittered before windows spread with Madeira embroidery, with drawn-work handkerchiefs, with Japanese kimonos showing vivid flashes of tomato-red linings, with silk and crêpe de Chine lingerie in pink and orchid and rose.

"There's a pretty one. Look, Carrie. . . . No, not that one. The third on this side, with the two-toned ribbon. That would look good on you."

"I'm too dark for orchid."

"I used to wear it when I was a girl your age. I remember I had a waist, time I was engaged, trimmed with this passementerie across here in a kind of a yoke—that was when they wore basques———"

"Oh, come on! What do you girls want to stand looking at that stuff all day for? Good gosh, I got a notion to go on by myself if you don't stop gawping in front of every window you see."

It was queer how remote the ocean seemed. You hardly noticed it at all lying out there so flat and blue-gray. Perhaps it was because of the people passing, repassing, marching up and down, up and down, like dream figures up and down, or sitting fatly swathed in wheel chairs with grotesquely bent black gnomes toiling flatfootedly behind. Canes, post cards, balloons, salt-water taffy, nut fudge, souvenirs, get-your-picture-taken-in-two-minutes.

They had their late luncheon at one of the restaurants on the Boardwalk. "Dinner at the hotel's all right," said Pa Cowan, "but no use throwing good money away for lunch. They charge you twice as much in a hotel dining room as they do here, and the food's no better if as good and no service at all unless you tip like a drunken sailor."

They walked back to their hotel. The old man abandoned his springy stride. He was frankly weary, as was his wife. The Madeira embroidery and the souvenirs and the kimonos and the new spring models were much less interesting when you passed them a second time. Mrs. Cowan and Carrie did not stop more than twice on the return walk.

"We'll take a chair this afternoon," said Ma Cowan. "I've done all the walking I want for one day."

"Call this a walk!" scoffed Pa Cowan. But his eyes looked fagged.

"I certainly do. And I'm going right up to the room and have a nap and so are you. It wouldn't hurt you to lie down either, Carrie."

Carrie shook her head. "I'm going to wrap up and sit out on the porch in the sun. Why don't you lie down in my room, and Pa in yours? You'll rest better."

They separated to meet again at half-past three. From half-past three until five up and down in a wheel chair, almost to the Inlet and back. Up and down, up and down swam the dream figures, marching, riding. Madeira embroidery, balloons, kimonos, post cards, salt-water taffy. And there beyond, the flat blue-gray expanse that was the ocean.

Pa Cowan remarked it. "I don't ever remember seeing the ocean as quiet as it is to-day. Look at that!" He waved a patronizing arm. "Flat as a mill pond. You forget it's there, that's a fact."

They talked little. They had little to say to each other. They spoke disconnectedly, fragmentarily.

"This air certainly makes you sleepy. Funny, though. Laid down and never closed an eye."

"I see those plain tailored mannish suits are coming back."

"That was Gloria Dalton we just passed! It was too. I'd know her anywhere. She looks a lot older than she does on the screen, though."

"Getting pretty chilly now, towards evening. Let's have him turn around. I guess I'll get out and walk awhile."

"You've walked enough, Pa."

Carrie and her mother dressed for dinner, Mrs. Cowan in her faille crêpe and Carrie in her sleeveless black velvet. The dining room was etched with sleeveless black velvets.

"Yours looks as good as anybody's," said Mrs. Cowan. "And it's last year's too."

"A good black velvet's always good."

The orchestra lent an air of gaiety, but the diners were solemn and constrained. Americans taking their holiday heavily. Carrie cut loose a bit and ordered hors-d'œuvres of sea food, braised celery, shad roe, chocolate meringue. "Things I don't get at home." But Ma and Pa Cowan were cautious, as they had been at luncheon. They ordered accustomed dishes. The old man had scant chance to do otherwise under his wife's watchful eye. For nineteen years a chronic ailment had made sweets, starches, and red meats forbidden delights for him. Mrs. Cowan made quite a ritual of his white meat of chicken, his spinach, his stewed fruit and sawdust-like biscuits. Sometimes he rebelled, but the revolt always came to nothing.

"Now you know you can't touch that stuff," she would caution him. "It's poison for you."

"I just wanted to taste it."

"No. If you're hungry you'll——"

"I'm sick and tired of this stuff."

But she was firm, vigilant, inexorable. "You know who'll suffer for it. You're like a child."

Indeed he did resemble a naughty child as he sat at table, sulking, rebellious, greedy.

After dinner there was little to do except sit in the rococo lounge with the other sleeveless black velvets and listen to the orchestra and comment and speculate on the others sitting so stiffly about on the massive and ridiculous couches.

"I'll bet she's never married to him."

"Look at that. Isn't that terrible! And I suppose she thinks she looks grand."

Pa Cowan shook himself impatiently. "What do you say we go to a movie? I noticed there's one just a few steps down. Can't sit here all evening, and it's too early to go to bed."

They saw the picture. They often went to the pictures in Newark and were glib and expert in their criticism. The picture was taken from a classic with a mediæval setting full of iron doors and turrets, and winding stairways and spears and doublets and oak-beamed halls. It gave the star an opportunity to wear pearl-encrusted robes, and be rescued from the slimy monarch, and let down her golden hair, and ride on a milk-white palfrey, and sit on a chair with a Gothic back, all robed in cloth of gold and velvet and ermine, and change to the ragged tattered georgette crêpe of a beggar maid. The picture had cost seven hundred thousand dollars. The Cowans viewed it with coldly critical eyes. When they emerged

nto the lights of the Boardwalk they said that it was
a pretty fair picture.

The old man and old woman in their room and the
middle-aged spinster in hers slept well after their half
day in the salt air. But they awoke at their accustomed
early hour and could not sleep again.

"You up, Carrie?"

"Yes."

"It's only seven-thirty."

The day stretched empty ahead of them. Walk.
Wheel chair. Windows. Some desultory shopping.
Madeira embroidery, post cards, salt-water taffy.

Mrs. Cowan stopped again before the window full of
pink and rose and orchid crêpe de Chine. "I think that
orchid set is lovely. I wonder how much it is."

"What do you want to know for?"

"Oh, I'd just like to know. For fun. Wait a minute."
She entered the shop—came out again uninformed.
'The woman says it's to be auctioned off this afternoon
with a lot of other sets, and table linen, and lace."

"Well, I don't see——" said Carrie vaguely. The
truth is she was bored. So was Ma Cowan bored. So was
Pa Cowan bored. Bored with Atlantic City, with the
Madeira embroidery and post cards, with each other;
with walking; with riding in wheel chairs; with the flat
blue-gray ocean and the seaside sunshine so hard and
brilliant and false.

"Great stuff, this sea air," Pa Cowan still said from
time to time, but his heart wasn't in it.

By noon they were snapping at each other irritably.
Well, what do you want to do, then? Well, why didn't

you say so in the first place? Lunch? Pa Cowan didn't think he'd eat any lunch. No, he felt all right. Felt fine. But he had had breakfast at nine instead of at his accustomed hour of seven-thirty. He had eaten two eggs. The man had brought him two. Simply wasn't hungry, that's all. No use stuffing yourself if you're not hungry.

"Do you want to sit with us while we eat? Ma and I'll have a sandwich and a cup of tea in one of these tea rooms."

No, he didn't think so. Just sitting there at the table. There was an exhibit up the Walk a ways that he wanted to take in. Showed how they made Happy Days cigarettes. Not a human hand touched 'em. Everything by machinery—rolling, packing, labelling—everything. He turned to go.

"We-e-ell," said Ma Cowan, reluctantly, doubtfully. "You sure you feel all right?"

"Never felt better in my life. See you at the room later." He was off briskly. There was a new lift to his shoulders, almost a spring in his step. His faded old eyes burned momentarily with the light of anticipated adventure. He actually did go to the white painted building in which you saw all the processes in the mechanical birth of Happy Days cigarettes. He had said he was going and he went. But by one o'clock he had struck off down a side street away from the Boardwalk and toward the business district of the city. He went at a brisk pace, his face almost grim with determination. The light of daring—of adventure—was now aflame in his eyes. "Got shut of those womenfolks," he said to himself with satisfaction. He stopped a passer-by to ask: "Can you tell me the name of a first-class restaurant or lunch room in town?"

"I'm a stranger here myself," said the man.

Pa Cowan continued his walk, away from the ocean and toward the business section. He'd find something. He walked spryly. The streets were busy here. More like Newark. Street cars and trucks and traffic policemen. On a window, in fat raised white lettering, he read, "Steaks, Chops, Oysters." In the window, nestling amongst the crisp greenery of lettuce frills, Pa Cowan saw the red and white of forbidden foods. He entered.

"Um—bring me a steak," he said to the waitress. "Cut thick." He indicated a surprising thickness with thumb and forefinger.

"That's what we call an extra steak," said the girl. "Cost you dollar and a half."

"I didn't ask what it would cost," retorted Old Man Cowan testily. "An order of French fried. Got some lima beans? All right. With butter. Cup of coffee. Afterwards you can bring me piece of that chocolate layer cake I saw in the case up in front. Uh, make it a pot of coffee, you'd better." He sat waiting for his meal, fumbling with napkin, with salt shaker, breaking up matches from the little white china holder. The hands with the brownish splotches on the backs shook a little.

The girl brought rolls and butter, filled his glass with water. "Some oysters while you're waiting? Steak'll take about fifteen minutes."

"No." There was a dash of unwonted pink in the lean old cheeks. He broke off a piece of roll, buttered it, pushed it away. He would not dull the keen edge of this adventure.

The girl came with his laden tray. She placed the steak before him. "Is that the way you like it? You didn't say, but I told chef medium. Is that all right?"

He prodded it with his knife. "That's fine. Fine.'

As he munched the forbidden food he resembled in a startling degree a naughty boy, his eyes darting here and there as though even in this remote corner he was not safe from Ma's watchful scrutiny. He devoured all the monstrous meal. He drank the hot, stimulating coffee with plenty of cream and sugar. He glanced carelessly at his check, left an almost ostentatious tip for the girl, stopped at the cashier's desk near the door, took a paper-sheathed toothpick from the little glass holder. He felt rakish, free, expansive, wicked. The cashier was a cool and insolent blonde. The wave of her hair, the glitter of her nails, the toss of her earrings, the carmine of her lips proclaimed her aloofness from such poor things as Pa Cowan. The size of his check as he paid it brought no flicker of interest into the disdainful face. And yet Pa Cowan, bursting with beef and buoyancy, had the temerity to address this splendid one airily, thus:

"Well, m' girl, I guess that five-dollar bill will look pretty sick time you get through with it." He picked up his change. "Fine weather you're giving us visitors."

The girl disregarded him with a cold blue eye. Her look did not spell active dislike. It was too remote even for disfavour. Still, she was not a vindictive person; and weather conversation was, after all, one of the duties of an Atlantic City dweller. People—visitors—talked to you about the weather and you answered automatically. They expected it. She answered now.

"Yeh."

Pa Cowan emerged from the portals of sin, satisfied. He thought with some distaste of going back to his hotel. He had no intention of confession. But he had Ma to face, and Ma had a curious trick of finding things out. Pa Cowan hated unpleasant family scenes. He hated to be caught in some petty crime by his wife. On such occasions she spoke of him to his daughters as "your father."

The room reached, Ma Cowan was not there. Neither, on further investigation, was Carrie in her room. Out on the sun porch, probably. He was drowsy in spite of the unaccustomed coffee. He settled himself for a nap. As he dozed off he had the queer idea that two hundred-pound weights of iron had settled themselves on his chest.

He had been right about Carrie. Supine in a steamer chair, swathed in a rug, Carrie lay in the watery spring sunshine on the hotel veranda, sheltered from the breeze. She was holding a book which she did not read, and she was thinking: "I suppose this is doing me good, out in the fresh air all day like this. . . . Good—for what? Suppose it is! Then what? . . . I wish . . . No wonder Evelyn's so nice to Daisy, with that brother-in-law . . . Poor Ev. A pretty bum time she has anyway, lumped in there with us . . . I'll be glad to get back to-morrow. . . . What's Ma doing, I wonder? Sleeping? . . . I'll be old, too, in a few years now and I've never lived a minute."

She shut her eyes, but not in sleep.

Down in the baths on the second floor —separate departments for men and women—Ma Cowan, alarmingly red of face, was seated in a white enamelled electric bath cabinet, her head sticking out of the round hole in the top, for all the world like a guillotine victim on exhibition. The bath attendant, a plump, dark-haired, eye-glassed woman with a good-natured face and strong, spatulate fingers, was leaning sociably against the cabinet, watching its temperature indicator warily even while she appeared not to. She had seen these stout old women go off into a sudden faint when they weren't used to bath cabinets. Ma Cowan was confiding in her. Patients always confided in her. She could hear without listening, thinking the while of many other things. Ma Cowan talked on.

"And another thing I always wanted to do was take a bath like this and a massage. But you know how it is. You think you'll do a thing and then you never get around to it. I've always had a kind of full figure and if I could have done the way lots of other women do, take massage and baths regular——"

"Don't you think you'd better come out now?" said the woman. "You've been in fifteen minutes and over. Usually we don't——" She regarded Ma's plump purple face a little anxiously. "You feeling all right?"

"Grand. I love it. I can just feel myself getting thin. How much do people usually lose in a treatment like this?"

"Well," said the woman, "half a pound or so."

"Imagine! Half a pound, and no effort. Time I was

married to Mr. Cowan I had quite a nice figure. Real trim. They wore those tight-fitting things then and I could carry them off to perfection. Those days hips were natural and not something to be ashamed of."

"Don't you think you'd better come out now?" She flicked off a knob that controlled one set of lights within the cabinet.

"I'll sit here just another minute with the heat off. It's funny how I came to take this bath. I saw the sign up in my bathroom advertising them. I was just going to take a nap. And I thought to myself, why couldn't I treat myself to something I'd always wanted to do? I guess what I had done before started it. Don't you get the funniest wild notions when you're on a holiday? I sneaked off from my daughter Carrie who's here with me, and I bought an orchid silk set—nightgown and step-ins and petticoat—that I'll never wear. An old woman like me. But I've always wanted one. When I was married they never heard of such a thing as crêpe de Chine underwear. My land, no! Muslin with ruffles of embroidery, and high-necked, long-sleeved nightgowns. My married daughter Evelyn doesn't have any sleeves at all in hers. That is, she was married. She's a widow now. I don't know what I'll do with the set. Give it to her probably. Another thing I always wanted was a red silk dress. I think dark women in red always——"

"You'd better come out now," said the attendant, firmly. She wrapped Ma Cowan in a sheet and the treatment proceeded. Soaping, hosing, shower, massage. Ma Cowan bulked huge on the flat table. The treatment ended, she was weighed. Happiness radiated her. "I've lost half a pound!" and she stepped down from the scales, shaking the room as she did so. It was as though a mountain were to rejoice because a pebble had rolled down from its peak.

Up in her room she found Pa sound asleep and breathing stertorously. She lay down in Carrie's unoccupied room, feeling delightfully languid and drowsy. She thought of the orchid crêpe de Chine set in the bottom of her suitcase.

Carrie, coming in at five, found them both still asleep. Ma had started up at her entrance, but Pa had actually to be shaken before he could be roused. Both of them, as the lights were turned on, looked queer. Ma's face was very red and she said she felt as though she had one of her headaches coming on. Pa's face was drawn and strangely yellow—golden almost, and with a greenish tinge.

"Don't you feel well?" the two women asked him.

"Sure. I feel all right. Why shouldn't I? Slept too long, I guess. Foolish. Come here to Atlantic City and spend a lot of money for rooms and all and then sleep your time away."

At dinner he looked queerer than ever. He ate nothing though he ordered almost defiantly. For that matter Mrs. Cowan looked queer too, with her flushed face and her bloodshot eyes. "I'm just going to have a plate of soup," she said. "My head's beginning."

No one suggested going to see a picture to-night. They sat again in the lounge.

"I'd like to take a walk," said Carrie.

"You don't want to walk alone. And I've had all the

walking I can stand. I'm going to bed early, with this head of mine."

"I'm going now," said Pa Cowan suddenly. He got up. "Man at the door says it's turned rough out. And a fog. Says there'll probably be a storm by to-morrow."

Mrs. Cowan sat a half-hour longer with her daughter. Then she succumbed. "I'm dead. I've got to go up. You don't want to sit here alone, do you, Carrie?"

"A little while. Until the music stops. I'll be up. I'll read in bed. I never get a chance to at home."

She sat there alone in a corner of the great couch. Little groups sat all about. Men and women talking, smoking, relaxed, companionable. Carrie sat alone, watching them with hot eyes. The orchestra was playing that thing that Bordoni sang—"So This Is Love." The musicians were not particularly gifted, but the violinist had the trick of making his instrument wail. When the piece was finished the room seemed suddenly peopled with ghosts. Carrie rose and went up to her room.

"Getting rough," said the splendid elevator attendant, looking like a glorified Coldstream Guard.

Carrie went into her own room. She heard her mother moving about next door. She opened the connecting door and stood a moment in the doorway. As she did so her mother thrust something hastily out of sight, turned toward her, her face redder than ever.

"My land, you scared me to death! I didn't hear you come in." She was in kimono and slippers. She nodded toward the bed. "He's sleeping again. He was asleep when I came in and here it's only ten o'clock." The old man was breathing heavily.

"Out of doors so much," said Carrie vaguely. "Good-night." She shut the door. She undressed slowly, washed some silk stockings, creamed her nails and the little fine lines under her eyes. Once in bed she picked up the book that had failed to hold her in the afternoon. She read a page or two with her eyes only.

Suddenly she found herself listening. She was conscious of listening to something like a slow and regular drum-beat. Beat—beat—beat—went something pulselike, insistent. The sea. The great gray-blue waste that had irritated her so by day lying there beyond the Boardwalk, so flat and smooth, like a back drop in a theatre. It had made her restless and moody. And now suddenly it had wakened. Boom—boom—boom. A drum, calling her. She turned out her bed light and went to the window in her bare feet. She shaded her eyes with her cupped hands and looked out. Strange how much nearer it seemed from her high window than it had been when she was passing it by day and on a level with it. Now, a great black beast, it lay below her window, calling to her.

She went back to bed. Lay there, listening. She found herself timing this pulsing sound with the beat of her own heart. She shut her eyes, very wide awake. Boom. Boom. Boom. Surging that fused with her heart. Between beats she could hear the unlovely sounds—those chokings, splutterings, inhalations, exhausts, and whistles—which marked her father's tryst with the nocturnal fairy. She listened closer to catch the sound of her mother's quieter breathing—that indomitable woman, her mother.

She lay there a moment longer. Then she got up quietly and dressed without turning on the light. She put on her long cloth coat and her round felt hat. She was very cunning and deft about it, as though she were in the habit of stealing out at night—as though for days, for years, she had planned this slipping out at night— as perhaps she had. Fully dressed, she began to open her door slowly, slowly, timing each turn of the knob and widening of the crack with the beat—beat—beat of the drum. Softly, softly. Sometimes the beat of the drum and the terrific snore from the next room came at the same time. She made great headway when this happened. She was out! She was out in the red-carpeted corridor. She pressed the elevator button. When the door was flung open she was a little afraid to face the surprise of the blue and gold and scarlet Coldstream Guard. But he evidently found nothing unusual in the sight of this plain woman in her heavy dark coat and small close hat bound for a walk at eleven at night. His flat, tapering back unbent just a little.

"Out for a nightcap?" said this splendid creature.

"Nightcap?"

"Yeh. 'S what we call a late stroll on the Walk to make you sleep."

"Oh, yes!" said Carrie gratefully. "Yes. I couldn't get to sleep."

"'S the best time, now is, when the crowd is gone and you got the works to yourself."

The door was flung splendidly open. She was out. Pearly gray chiffon veiled the Walk, the ocean, the lights, the great turreted hotels. Fog. And beyond it the beat of the drum. A gold and mauve aura hung about each street lamp. The Walk was black and slippery with moisture.

She began to walk briskly away from the hotel. She breathed deeply, feeling suddenly free, exhilarated, happy, almost young. The Atlantic City of the daylight —the shops, the Madeira embroidery, the balloons, the post cards, the salt-water taffy, the Japanese kimonos, the dream people swimming up and down, up and down —all had vanished. Now there was only the ocean and the fog. The drum beat and the banner. She walked perhaps a mile, happily. She turned, came back. Her cheeks felt fresh and cool, as though colour had been whipped into them. Her eyes felt bright. She swerved suddenly and went to the railing that separated walk from beach. She leaned on her folded arms, staring out into the blackness—beyond. Boom—boom—boom. Come—come—come. You—you—you.

"Cer'nly is some foggy night," said a voice beside her. A man's voice. "God pity the lads at sea on a night like this, say I." He laughed a little uncertainly.

A tall man. Broad-shouldered. A rakish cap pulled down over his eyes. A great overcoat. The scarlet eye of a cigarette blinking down at her. Carrie laughed too, and was surprised to hear her own laugh. She looked up at him, again faced the ocean, waited. Well, this was what happened to you when you walked alone on the Boardwalk in Atlantic City at midnight. And why not? She waited as an experienced woman would have waited. Something told her that this was the thing to do.

"Out alone, girlie?"

Girlie. "Yes. I came out for a little nightcap."

"Say, that's a good one. You're a card. Nightcap. That's a new one." He laughed appreciatively. His shoulder in the great rough coat just touched her arm. She did not move away. "That's a great little idea, I'll say."

"Nobody else seems to have thought of it," said Carrie. "I walked almost a mile and hardly met a soul."

"Afraid of the fog, I guess. I like it. The foggier the better. Give me a foggy night and a strange road and my car to drive and I'm happy. Some hate it, but not me."

"Oh, I don't know about driving in the fog!" How easy it was, this conversation. His car. He probably didn't have one. Just talk.

"Like to try it?"

"Try it? How do you mean?"

"Take a little run to-night in the fog. I know a little place between here and Philly where we can get something——"

She felt a little breathless. She must have time. "Are—are you from Philadelphia?"

"Among other places. Florida, Philadelphia, California, Europe. A few of the places I'm from. Where're you from, girlie?" He leaned closer. She did not move away.

Newark. She could not bring herself to say Newark. Not after Florida, California, Europe. "I'm from New York."

"Yeh? New York's all right if you like it." They were silent a moment. "Say, that hat certainly's got me stumped. How can I tell whether you're a blonde or a brunette with that hat down over your head like that?"

"Perhaps it's just as well," said Carrie, and laughed. "Which do you like?"

"Brunette," said the man.

Carrie pulled off her hat and laughed up at him, her head thrown back, her face sparkling. "I aim to please," she retorted. Suddenly, swiftly, the great rough coat sleeve was about her. The man leaned down, breathing queerly, almost sobbingly. He kissed her. A long kiss. And Carrie's mind, working clearly, said: "So this is it. Well, I don't even like it. It feels as if I had fallen face down into a plate of wet sausages."

She jerked herself free.

"You're not sore, are you, girlie?"

"No." She put on her hat.

"Come on, take a ride with me in the fog. A night-cap." He laughed.

"Where's your car?"

"In the garage. It'll only take a minute. If you'll wait for me at the foot of this street——"

"I don't believe you've got a car."

"Don't believe! Why, say, come along with me to the garage, then. What do you think I drove to Atlantic City in? What do you think I'm going to Florida in next Tuesday, huh?"

"I'll come to the garage with you."

She was not at all clear in her mind as to her future course of action. Not that it mattered. Too careful all her life, that was the trouble with her. You had to meet things halfway.

The garage was a great cavern in which rubber-booted giants armed with hose and sponge were slaves to steeds of steel and enamel. She waited, a little fearfully, in the doorway. The man seemed taller, more masterful than ever now. He strode over to a huge and powerful car whose hooded engine loomed enormous under the garage lights.

"Taking the bus out," she heard him say to one of the men. "How's she fixed for gas?" And then something about valves and carbon. The garage attendant lifted the hood. Together the two men peered in. She could not hear what the garage man was saying. The noise of the hose, suddenly turned on a car, drowned his utterance. What he said was: "You taking out that skirt? Say, your boss finds out you been joy-riding again in the car I bet he fires you. He was shooting off this morning only about where had the gas went to that was put in yesterday."

"Shut up!" said the other, and climbed into the driver's seat as the mechanic clamped the hood.

As she saw this, terror possessed Carrie; and with terror reason returned to her. He pressed the starter. The car began to throb gently. Without a last backward glance Carrie turned, fled, flew up the short street to the Boardwalk.

"Well," said the elevator man—oh, the dear, accustomed elevator man in his friendly homely blue and gold and scarlet!—"you must of had quite a walk at that."

"Yes. Quite a walk." She could even smile.

She unlocked her door gently, gently, timing the

sounds again with the beats of the far-away drum. She opened her door. Her room was flooded with light. So, too, was the room seen just beyond. Her mother, in a kimono, was standing in the middle of the room. She was looking very wild and old and vast. A strange man, cool and competent and eye-glassed, stood at the bedside.

"Your father! He's been terribly sick. I thought he was dying. I don't know what—I had my headache and woke up all of a sudden and heard him breathing funny ——" She stopped, regarded Carrie piercingly. "Where've you been, Carrie Cowan, I'd like to know? This time of night! And your father almost dying!"

Carrie took off her hat. Little drops of moisture, born of the fog, beaded her hair, her lashes. Her cheeks were pink. "I couldn't sleep. I took a walk. I——" Terror shook her. She went to the bed. An old, old man looked up at her with eyes that had known recent and terrible anguish. "Pa! Pa, you all right now?" She felt a sudden rush of tenderness toward him, so yellow and frail and suffering. The old man nodded; even attempted a grimacing smile.

"I'm fine. Never felt better in my life. Must have et something didn't agree with me, that's all."

"It's those two eggs," said Ma Cowan, "for breakfast." He looked at her gratefully.

The strange man at the bedside finished writing on a little pad. "I'll just leave this to be filled on my way down and the bellboy will bring it up. He'll be all right now. Won't you, sir? That's right. Only don't do that again, young man." He smiled with professional cheerfulness at the drawn old face on the pillow.

"Can we go home to-morrow?" inquired Ma Cowan, fearfully. "Will he be able?"

"I think so. I think so. I'll look in at about ten to-morrow morning."

He was gone. The old woman came to the bedside, put one plump hand on the lean shoulder under the bedclothes. "You scared my headache away," she said. She turned suddenly to where Carrie stood, drooping. "Crazy thing for you to do. Run out at this hour the night. What possessed you to do a thing like that?"

Carrie touched the crown of her hat with her forefinger. The hat was damp. She looked down at it dully. "Oh, I don't know! You think of foolish things on a holiday that you wouldn't do at home. You get a kind of crazy feeling."

The old man stirred in the bed. The old woman put a hand to her head absently, as though the headache had not after all quite vanished.

By three next day they were back in Tichenor Street, Newark, these holiday seekers. Evelyn welcomed them. The children, Dorothy and Junior, fell upon their balloons and post cards and salt-water taffy with shouts and boundings. Evelyn, called to the telephone ten minutes after their return, could hardly hear for the noise.

"Hello! . . . Oh, it's you, Daisy . . . Yes, it was nice. I'm glad you enjoyed it . . . Uh, not now. Not now. Yes, they're just back . . . They say they had a fine time.

(Junior, you oughtn't to eat that taffy with your brace. You'll break it as sure as anything.) . . . Oh, well, I suppose they didn't do anything they couldn't do at home, but it's the—(Sister, you mustn't sit on Lover's balloon. No. No! *No*, I say!) . . . She's sitting on Junior's balloon and I just know . . . I was saying it's the change that does you good. I don't care about Atlantic myself. Just the ocean and taffy and post cards and those hotels and Madeira embroid—— (There! I knew it! Don't cry now. It won't do you any good to cry now. Mother warned you.)"

Consider the Lilies

CONSIDER
THE LILIES

Edna Ferber

CONSIDER THE LILIES

CLYBOURN AVENUE has a rather elegant sound. There never was a more inelegant thoroughfare. To learn how completely inelegant it is you have but to immerse yourself for one brief dip into that welter and boiling which is the intersection of Clybourn Avenue, Halsted Street, and North Avenue, Chicago. The Clybourn Avenue street cars, flat-wheeled, crash up and down bearing swarthy men with dinner pails and hatless women hugging lumpy brown paper bundles. The three-story flats and the sooty wooden houses lean sociably against butcher shops with unsavoury entrails in the windows, drug stores displaying trusses, and furniture emporiums whose taffy-coloured bedroom sets are marked in plain dollars and cents. Ninety-eight cents is a favourite figure in Clybourn Avenue.

It isn't a disreputable neighbourhood, nor one of poverty. Its residents are, for the most part, foreign-born labourers—a "Hunky" neighbourhood, Chicagoans will tell you—by which they mean, in this case, Hungarian. Placards and playbills of the district bristle with strange accent marks and umlauts and distorted words like Budapesti and Chicagoban. So the street was twenty years ago. So it is to-day, except, perhaps, that the front has been clawed out of an occasional butcher shop to disclose the equally sanguine wares of a motion picture palace.

Twenty years ago this Clybourn Avenue, itself none too prim, pronounced Poli Zbado a wild one. By this the neighbourhood did not mean that she was a bad girl. She wasn't. What they actually meant—and said— was: "That Zbado's Poli, she's a crazy *tzigane*." When you've said that—on Clybourn Avenue—you've said everything. A *tzigane* is a Hungarian gipsy. And a Hungarian gipsy—well, if you are Hungarian, and live on Clybourn, and have a little *tzigane* blood in you, you do not brag about it. For while everyone knows that the *tzigane* orchestra makes the most bewitching and pulse-stirring music, and that the *tzigane* of comic opera minstrelsy, in velvet pants and vivid sash, is a dashing and popular figure, he is not, by practical people, con-sidered an asset as an ancestor. In fact, the term has come to be an opprobrium: "Crazy as a *tzigane*— thieving as a *tzigane*—wild as a *tzigane*."

The Zbados, as a family, were a hard-working, decent enough lot, of the foreign-born labouring class, and having no ambition to step out of it. At the age of three Poli had been brought to America by Pa and Ma Zbado from one of that long string of Hungarian hamlets called Három Revuca—the Three Revucas. They brought also other young Zbados of assorted ages, not to mention Grandma Zbado, aged Heaven only knew what. All of them made straight for Clybourn Avenue and a job, and got it—that is, they all got a job except Poli, of course, who wasn't quite expected to work at the age of three.

In numbers the family was out of all arithmetical proportion to the space it occupied (three rooms, rear). Still, you rarely found them all at home at once; and Poli, that wild one, was practically never home. They all worked and saved and prospered. Pa Zbado, being a mechanic, was employed at a place appropriately designated as "the works." Ma Zbado, naturally, washed and scrubbed in other people's households, her own being administered by Grandma Zbado. All the young Zbados—always excepting Poli—worked. The inevitable roomer worked at night and occupied a Zbado bed in the daytime.

So from morning until night the three rooms were empty—or comparatively empty. Only the roomer snoring hideously in his corner; Grandma Zbado padding heavily about her cooking or washing or scrubbing; and the *al fresco* Poli coming in for an occasional hunk of food. For from three to seventeen—when she married Tony Sebok and became an incredibly settled matron with a respectably shapeless figure and her hair in crimpers—Poli Zbado roamed the streets of Chicago's north side when she should have been at school or at home or at work.

Poli's gipsying was urban, perforce, but it satisfied an urge. Four walls irked her. When a grind-organ appeared in Clybourn Avenue she followed it for miles and was usually restored to an unperturbed family by a harassed-looking policeman with scratches on his hands. "There! Take her!" he would say, "and welcome— the little wildcat she is." Poli's shoe laces would be untied, her black hair stringing all about her gipsy face, and that face a tragi-comic mask of Chicago dirt, pilfered food, and tears of temper.

In the storm of gutturals that ensued the policeman would make his escape, muttering and nursing his hand. Though the babel in the Zbado kitchen sounded like a riot, he was wiser than to call the wagon. Twelve years patrolling the district had taught him that any language composed almost entirely of crowded consonants, with a *c* and a *b* and a *z* actually making up one syllable, is likely to sound explosive when uttered under emotion; and that Ma Zbado, instead of threatening infanticide, as would appear from the sounds she made, was merely saying in maternal Hungarian: "Where have you been, you little bum, you! You crazy gipsy! Look at your clothes! Sit down, now, and eat your supper."

If the motion picture had obtained in Poli's childhood she might have found vicarious relief in witnessing the perils and escapes of its celluloid heroines. But the best that Clybourn Avenue of twenty years ago had to offer her was a barker selling his wares under a street-corner gas flare. Perhaps he had nothing more romantic to sell than a polisher for pots, pans, and sink faucets. But Poli would press eagerly into the circle surrounding this leisurely talking, confident stranger.

"It will not scratch"—pause—"rub"—pause—"or warsh off. Re-moves vurdygreeze."

Poli would stare unblinking at the glitter of the gas flare on his wares. She would finger the little bottles with their strange coloured liquids, and the bits of shining metal. "Kindly put that down, young lady, unless you intend to purchase." Poli would make a horrible face at him, but stand her ground until he moved on. Purchasing was far from her desire or power. The wares themselves did not interest her, except as colour, as magic. That which fascinated her was the mystery and impermanency of the whole nomadic outfit—man, cart, gas flare, stock in trade. Here to-night and gone to-morrow. Another street corner, another crowd, another town, perhaps. That was the life.

Of all the decent, hard-working Hungarian household, the old grandmother crone at one end and the little witch Poli at the other were the outlaws. For Grandma Zbado had her memories, and these, confided to Poli alone, probably had much to do with that one's nomad-ism. Clybourn Avenue did not exist for the old woman slip-slapping about the crowded flat. Street cars, police-men, plumbing, gaslight, hot and cold water, meat wrapped in brown-paper parcels, pay checks brought home on Saturday night—what meaning had these for her who had known broad moors; purple mountains; copper-bronze bodies in the camp-fire light; wooden huts against a sheltering rock; blood-red berries plucked off a thorny hedge; slumber in a copse of young birch trees that were like slender maidens with long floating hair swaying in the breeze!

She could have told you of one gipsy girl who had married a young Slovak and who had run away from his house to sleep in the woods. Sometimes she used strange words: *Vagda; Gako;* Velvet Georgie.

"Tell me how they made the bear learn to dance,"

Poli would command. Grandma Zbado would push the little black shawl back from her head, champ her old gums, and begin:

"To make him learn to dance they put the young bear on a thin piece of iron that was hot. Hot! Then on the fiddle the *tzigane* would play music. Music like this— *zoom*—*zoom*—*zoom*—like you would keep time with heavy beats. The sheet of iron is very hot and the bear lifts his legs, first one leg high and then the other because of the heat. And always he is hearing the time marked by the music, though he does not know this. But afterward, whenever he hears the *tzigane* begin to play that tune on the fiddle, the bear remembers the hot iron and he lifts his feet, first one and then the other. So he is the dancing bear."

Poli's dark face would glow, little savage that she was. "That's fine! And now the toads."

"Oh, the toads! Well, when there is a fair in a village the *tzigane* comes because he has something to sell. He has a donkey, maybe, to sell. So he puts down the donkey's throat live toads. They move and jump around in his stomach and give him a fever, so that the donkey leaps around and looks lively and quick and the *tzigane* sells him for much money."

In Poli there stirred a vague consciousness of things she had never seen; smells she had never smelled; dark faces gleaming around a camp fire; the tinkle of armlets; the stamp of horses' hoofs on sod; the tantalizing savour of strange messes stewing in a great black pot.

Poli went to school, of course. She was likeliest to play truant on those October days when the pungent scent of burning leaves was in the air. The other small girls of the Hunky neighbourhood submitted graciously to the Anglicization of their names—urged it, even. So Bortscha became Bessie, Sari became Sarah, and Zsuzsi answered to Susie. But when the teacher said, smugly, "Poli? Uh-um—that's Pauline, isn't it? Pauline. Yes" —Poli would rise up, her shameless little skirts switching, her chin thrust forward, her dusky face blazing with the scarlet of resentment. In her thick tongue she mimicked as best she could the teacher's mincing speech.

"Paw-leen! Paw-leen! Naw! Me Poli! Poli Z-z-zbado!" She spat it out. Thumped her chest.

By the time she was sixteen Poli had had twenty jobs and twenty beaus and had been faithful to none of them. The truth was she wanted neither a job nor a husband. If she had been the modern girl of to-day she would have talked largely about freedom and self-expression and the development of the individual. But what she said, surveying her family's dutiful treadmill, was: "What do I want to work for all the time, or tie up to some man and work for him! Say, I want to—I want to——" The thing she wanted was so vague and yet so definite, so simple and yet so vastly unobtainable, that she herself could not name it. Fields. Skies. Distance. Travel. Freedom.

"Yeh, you want—you want!" scolded Ma Zbado, and quite properly. "You don't know what you want, crazy *tzigane*, you."

Poli's jobs had ranged all the way from factory to housework. Her suitors were, surprisingly enough—or

perhaps not so surprisingly—rather mild young Mag-
yars. Their wooings followed the conventional pattern
of the district—a quick grab and a quick rough kiss on
the part of the gentleman. A quicker slap from Poli.
The slap did not necessarily signify anger on the part of
the lady. It was little more than a polite and customary
maidenly gesture. But Poli usually meant it and thus
put more real vigour into it than the offender considered
quite ethical. He would smile the uncertain smile of surprise and real pain; his eyes smarting, he would bring
one calloused palm up to the tingling cheek. "Je's
Say, what you think! Crazy, you! A wild *tzigane!*"

"Hunky!" Poli would retort, none too elegantly.

Even a beauty must handle her suitors more graciously than that; and Poli was no beauty. With her
swarthy skin and her straight black hair she was not
considered handsome even by her male admirers; but
she had about her a sparkle, a zest, an impudent live-
liness. She travelled on a wave of buoyancy and carried
you with her. The flesh under her finger nails was dark,
with a lavender tint in it. Her cheek bones were high,
and the exaggerated socket made a setting that enhanced the catlike gleam of her eyes. The skin of her
arms and throat, though dusky, was smooth and had a
sort of dull sheen to it like that of a damson plum. You
wanted to touch it. You did touch it and got a stinging
slap. It was freely predicted by her family, her friends,
and her enemies—all numerous—that Poli Zbado would
come to a bad end. Always running the streets, going to
fortune tellers. A loafer. Always talking about the country. Who wanted to see the country? You could see

enough of it if you went northwest from Clybourn just
a half-hour's ride on the street car. Prairie and prairie
enough to make you sick.

At seventeen Poli met Tony Sebok at a Hungarian
dance at Prudential Hall. She was wearing a good many
red and green jewelled side combs in her hair and a pink
dress of a shade to bung your eyes out. Tony Sebok was
older than Poli by ten years. He had a walrus moustache
dark and fierce and dashing, and a pale blue satin neck-
tie and a bright blue suit, and was altogether a male
figure to please the feminine eye. All this was enhanced
by the fact that Tony himself made no further noticeable effort to win the girls to him. He was a widower.
Childless. Sober. Industrious, dependable, an expert
mechanic lately come to the neighbourhood from Pitts-
burgh and commanding a weekly wage larger than that
of the head of the Zbado household. A catch, if ever
there was one.

The luck of the unworthy was with Poli. The thing
was so simple as to be elemental. Every girl in the hall
learned that the widower's late wife had been pretty,
gentle, quiet, and virtuous and that he of the mustachios mourned her sincerely. So every girl in the hall at
once set about being a pattern of all that was pretty,
gentle, quiet, and virtuous. All, that is, except Poli. In
her red and green side combs and her lurid pink dress she
bounced and danced and laughed and pushed the boys
about and was pushed about by them. She danced the
sardas with such stampings and twirlings and clappings
as to make the others in the group look like frozen
figures on a Greek vase. The scarlet glowed beneath the

dusk of her cheeks, her eyes snapped, her coarse hair blew all about. The eyes of the bereaved one followed the pink figure all around the hall, as the pink figure was very well aware.

When finally they came together she called him Old Stick-in-the-Mud, in which she was quite justified considering that two weeks passed by before he kissed her for the first time. Poli was by then so worn with waiting that she barely had the spirit or good manners left to slap him. She just managed it, but you could see that her heart wasn't in it. He caught the hand that had slapped him, twisted it until she cried out in pain, pulled her to him and kissed her again. It was love, all right, this time.

"You got to save," said Tony, in exposition of his code of life, "and work, and get ahead, and bring up your family right."

"Sure," agreed Poli, made unbelievably meek by love. "Sure. That's how I always say."

They were married the following spring, and Poli Zbado, the wild one—the crazy *tzigane*—became Mrs. Tony Sebok, plump of figure, deft of hand, neat of hair, and settled down for twenty years. They took a little rear flat on North Avenue and prospered. You never would have suspected Poli Zbado in this comfortable matron who went marketing in the morning like the other wives of the neighbourhood in an overall apron, shoes run down at heel and hair in crimpers. Poli turned out to be a surprisingly excellent though haphazard cook. She was the kind who could "throw things in" and they came out right. Both she and Tony liked hot spicy

stewed messes—chicken or beef with plenty of tomatoes
and peppers and paprika and onion.

Punctuality was not one of Poli's virtues and they
quarrelled a good deal about her lack of it. When Tony
came home from the works at night he was as likely
as not to find his evening meal still to be made. But
when finally Poli did dump it deftly from pot to dish
and from dish to plate it was pretty sure to be hot,
stimulating, savoury. Tony's mustachios would emerge
dripping from bowl or cup. A sibilant indrawing of the
breath. "Is good," he would say.

"Yeh? Then for why you make such a holler!" But
into her face would flash that old sparkle for a moment.
That she still could manage a sparkle of any kind was
proof that the fire in Poli, though smothered and banked
for the moment by household and husband and children
—three living and one dead—was an enduring flame.

They quarrelled regularly and spiritedly enough, these
two, to keep life from being too even and dull. They
quarrelled and loved and had their children and lived
the existence of the American labouring class, which is
the most luxurious of any similar class in the world.
Phonograph, piano, pork roast, ice-cream cones, movies,
white kid shoes, silk shirts, cigars, chewing gum, plush
furniture, electric lights.

At intervals Poli had fits of sullen temper, of restless-
ness. At such times she and Tony were most likely to
quarrel. If Poli had belonged to another class she might
have said, "You don't *understand* me!" Instead, she
would go slamming and banging about the house, slap-
ping the children smartly, snapping at Tony, bickering

with the neighbours, setting the whole household by the ears with a whirlwind of scrubbing and dusting and polishing, or sitting moodily in a corner refusing to talk to any of them.

Tony, bewildered, would say, "What's eatin' you, anyway! Act like a looney." They spoke English now, or American, interlarded with pungent slang picked up from the children.

"Looney yourself. Might as well be dead, married to you. Settin' around all the time like a lump. Never go anywheres."

"Yeh, you always got to be running. Run—run—that's you. Never set still a minute. I come home tired, see? You laying around the house all day."

"You should of ought to of married a old stick-in-the-mud like you. They was plenty. I didn't want you. Slapped your face good the first time you come near me."

"Yeh, slapped! Liked to choked me the way you hung on to me."

"Wished I had of."

But they loved each other with the inarticulateness of their kind, and their very dissimilarity made an indissoluble bond between them long after their first passion had died. Following a quarrel such as this he would sit on the back porch or on the sidewalk in his stocking feet, smoking his evil-smelling pipe and spitting in a geometrical semicircle. She would run out into the neighbourhood somewhere and return late, to slam doors, bang bureau drawers, rattle pans maddeningly. Or she would dress next day in her white kid shoes, her satin hat and her lace waist and take the street car downtown, there to worm her way, perspiring, in and out of the crowded, odoriferous cheap stores on the wrong side of State Street, buying a sack of candy from the pile on the counter, eating a soda at the fountain, grabbing at remnants and ribbons and tumbled feathers and cotton flowers. She did not enjoy going downtown, but when she came home something in her seemed to have been satisfied. She would take off her unaccustomed corsets, get into roomy apron and slippers and serve Tony, on his arrival, a supper hot, appetizing, ample.

When first they were married, "Work, work!" she would sometimes say. "Person'd think that was all they was to living, just work, the way you and me do."

"Well, what else should you do! Work and save and bring up your kids right, that's the way, ain't it?"

The street cars roared and clanged by the house. The myriad street noises beat on the walls. Brick and stone.

"No, it ain't."

"Well, what is, then?"

"Oh, I dunno! Leave me alone, can't you!"

The four children had come with mathematical precision, one year apart. And Poli was twenty—she was twenty-five—she was thirty. Tony Sebok became a master mechanic. Seventy-seven cents an hour and time and a half for overtime. They had money in the bank on Halsted Street, and insurance papers. When georgette blouses trimmed with beads were shown in the Halsted department store Poli dripped beads like an Undine.

Tony had a chance to go into the Illinois Central

train shops, on the far south side, at an increase in wage. The district was known as Burnside and the prairies stretched all about. Sometimes you could not see a house for a mile. Then there would be a little cluster of workingmen's cottages. They built a little staring red excrescence of a bungalow that squatted in the midst of the open prairie. The two girls, Pauline and Emmy, and the boy, Louie, accustomed to the clangour of the crowded city streets, complained of the loneliness and threatened to leave home. Even Tony himself had a rather lost and wistful look, evenings, when the crickets were chorusing in the rank weeds and the clouds hung so low that sky and prairie seemed to be closing in all about them. But Poli was gayer than she had been in years. She snatched at any excuse to be out of doors. She used to stand on the neat little front porch staring out at the west where earth and sky met.

Tony, his stockinged feet on the porch rail, his pipe in his mouth, would regard her amusedly. "What you gawpin' at?"

"Huh? Oh, nothing. I was just wondering could you walk out to there where it's like a line coming together. I bet it's swell there."

"There! You talk crazy. There ain't nothing there only what's here. It's just like here."

"Yeh, what do you know! To the works and back, that's all you go."

There was a goodish tract of land behind the house which they used as a vegetable garden, but Poli worked there as little as possible. She was impatient of the weeding and hoeing and spading. Tony tended it evenings, after supper, or one of the children worked at it desultorily. Sometimes, on Sunday, they had a picnic. Poli was a picnic addict. She had always loved eating out of doors. She never seemed to mind the work, lugging the baskets and boxes of food on and off the crowded street cars and dragging them through the park to a shady cool spot. You saw her with Tony on summer Sunday afternoons with their own children and probably part of a neighbour's brood sprawled untidily on the grass in Jackson Park. Poli enjoyed these affairs enormously. She would spread her plump person on the ground and produce the viands and they would eat endlessly of the good food. Once or twice they had built a fire on the beach and had had hot "wieners" and corn and potatoes. Poli had been strangely exhilarated and gay.

She was thirty-five. She was nearing forty. It was incredible that twenty years could go whizzing by like that; that the bold black-haired girl in the crude pink dress that bunged your eye out was this stout, comfortable wife in a stylish ready-made dress and eight-dollar hat. Louie, the boy, was engine-wise, like his father. But no works for him. He drove a truck like a god in a juggernaut, sounding the siren devilishly in the ears of nervous and affrighted pedestrians, cutting out the muffler, swinging around corners in a death-defying curve, bawling at a traffic policeman who had reprimanded him. Louie was amazingly slim and hard and tough, but not bad. No walrus mustachios for him. A shave twice over to the blue. High belted suits evenings and Sundays, tan shoes, and a long-visored cap that came rakishly down over the eyes. He fooled around with Ma; came into the kitchen to filch food from pot or pan or pantry, stamped, whistled, sang, slammed out of the house. Poli pretended to scold him, but she liked it, and adored him. He had a girl and would marry any day, any hour. She had never seen the girl.

Pauline and Emmy married within six months of each other. Their wooing had been carried on comfortably in the warm, snug, dark intimacy of the motion picture palaces downtown. They had held hands with their boys while the hundred-thousand-dollar pipe organ sobbed and groaned and quavered, stirring their senses. They had married decent young mechanics and lived in bungalows of their own. They had cheap automobiles and visited Poli and Tony Sundays, often plumping their babies down and going off for the day.

The Seboks owned an automobile, too, as befitted a labouring man's family. Tony, with his knowledge of engines and of all things mechanical, had bought at a bargain a second-hand car of good make. He used the original car only as a basis on which to erect his own work of art. He knew the car's every part and improved on it. He worked on it as an artist on a canvas, bringing out a high light there, subduing a tone here. He could make it do incredible things. It was his slave, his toy. He usually drove to work in it, as did many of the other mechanics in the shops. You could note any day quite a covey of good-looking middle-class cars grouped in the cinder plot outside the shops. At five o'clock these streamed briskly out of the gates of the plant, driven by swarthy mustachioed men of Tony's age, their great work-grimed hands guiding the wheel expertly.

Poli loved the car. She would drop her work—whatever she was doing—to go riding in it. She usually donned for motoring a lace and ribbon atrocity known as a "boudoir cap." This intimate garment she wore in the gaseous crowded Chicago boulevards, her dark face all the darker in contrast with its absurd lacy frame. Sometimes, on Sundays, they "toured," whisking up and down the asphalted highways of the flat ugly Illinois prairie landscape; up and down, rather aimlessly, like thousands of others. Poli was happiest at such times.

So Poli and Tony Sebok approached middle age; overtook it. The house was paid for. They owned it; had improved it. Electric lights. A golden brown upright piano, bought on the instalment plan for the girls. Rugs in parlour and dining room. The ubiquitous radio. An almost human washing machine churned Tony's shirts and overalls clean. These belongings had marked the passing of the years. This year the piano. The next the washing machine. The next a new rug. The next the automobile. Eleven thousand dollars in the bank. Poli had worked hand in hand with him for all these things—had worked and saved and spent, as he had. And now—what? Work and save and bring up your kids right, Tony had said. Well, they had done these things. Now what?

Often, on summer evenings, they drove over to Jackson Park and drew up at the lake front. There they would sit, surveying with lack-lustre eye the calm or cavortings of the august body of water called Lake Michigan that stretched away to the horizon. Poli wore a neat summer dress and was hatless, urless adorned by the boudoir cap. Tony, in shirt-sleeves and suspenders, his feet propped up on the dashboard or fore door, spat judiciously and half dozed. Poli didn't care much for the water. She said it was kind of dumb, slopping around like that, going nowheres.

"I like a place where you can walk on it," she said. "A place where you can go if you want to, and build a fire and picnic, and like that."

Tony liked it. He would exchange pleasantries with the other men whose cars were parked slantwise on either side. He would smoke contentedly.

Suddenly Poli would give a little twitch and heave of her shoulders. "Le's go."

"We on'y just come."

"We been here a hour, anyway."

"Is nice here. What's the matter with it here?"

"Sittin' by the lake all night."

"Where you want to go to?"

"Oh, around. Driving around."

"What's always a-eatin' into you, anyway? Like a flea. By golly!"

Grumbling, he would start the car, slide it and twist it and back it deftly out of the line. Off they would go. Poli would draw a satisfied sigh. She usually talked little while they were driving.

Money in the bank; house; comfort; clothes; food; the children married.

"I wisht we could go somewheres different once," Poli said.

"We was to Elgin last Sunday on'y."

"Elgin!"

In July of that same summer came the strike at the shops. It was a foolish strike, and threatened to last the summer. It spread to South Chicago, to Gary. It was predicted that the familiar glow that you could see in the lowering, smoke-laden sky south of Chicago would be absent some night. That would mean catastrophe—the eternal fires in the great furnaces dead. Tony, level-headed, cool, experienced, was against the strike and said so.

One evening, a week later, a stone was thrown from a roadside covert, hitting him a nasty clip just behind the ear. It was a scalp wound, with profuse bleeding, but not a serious one. Poli was frantic. "See! That's what you get, shootin' off your mout'." But she hovered over him, would not let him out of her sight, fed him soup, scolded him tenderly.

The strike had been on three weeks, and no adjustment in sight. Tony was himself again, a little pale from the confinement. His great hands were strangely white, free of the shop grease and grit and grime. He spent hours in the little home-made garage back of the house, taking the car apart, greasing it, oiling it, polishing it.

Suddenly, one day, "Le's go somewheres," said Poli. "Not just around, I don't mean. Somewheres away. In the machine. What's the use stickin' around here, with them bums throwing stones and maybe guns, I bet, and the strike on I don't know for how long. Le's take the machine, me and you, and go somewheres on a trip. A far trip. A far ways."

Tony thought about it. He refused to commit himself.

Two days passed. Three. Then, at supper: "We could go to Youngstown, Ohio. To my brother Joe in Youngstown, on a visit."

Poli put down knife and fork. "Which way's that?" He pointed vaguely east. "No. I don't want to go that way. I want to go that way. Over there. Where I ain't never been. Over there." Poli pointed toward the west— toward the line where prairie and sky met. The horizon.

"That's west," Tony said.

"Aw' right. That's where I want to go. West."

Another week spent in tinkering the car and buying supplies. They got their routing though they seemed rather vague about their destination. "West," they replied to the question of the man at the office. "West." He gave them a dozen or more long pages of typed route list. The car, as they started out, bore strange protuberances on its sides and back; lumpy bundles and bales; queer shafts and poles strapped to the running boards; rolls of canvas on the fenders; boxes behind; bales and packages and yellow suitcases in the tonneau. So they started off, away from the smug bungalow and the well-ordered comfort of their labouring-class life, toward the horizon.

They struck out for the Lincoln Highway. At first they consulted their route instructions carefully; followed them meticulously. Jog right; left on Galena Avenue; right at foot of bridge; left at reverse fork; curve left. But as the days went on they developed a kind of road sense, an intuitive feeling for right or wrong that comes to the tourist, though they still held to their printed directions, of course. On toward the western orizon. At first they drove all day, sometimes fiercely, sometimes slowly, but maintaining a certain standard f miles daily. There was nothing relaxed about this driving. So many miles to Council Bluffs; so many miles o Omaha; so many miles to Lincoln, Nebraska.

"I guess we make this, how they call it—Wauneta— r, yes, that's how it is—Wauneta—to-night, huh?" oli would say.

"Naw, guess we push right on to this here Fort Mor- an. Feller back there to the filling station he tells me hey got a good camp ground there."

"Yeh?" She was satisfied. Just so they went on. itting there beside him, his great sure brown hands on he wheel, she would survey with dreamy catlike eyes he world spread ever anew before her. The flat prairies f the Iowa and Nebraska corn country found her still estless, fidgety.

At night they camped at public camping grounds. 'or the first thousand miles or so they clung automati- ally to the accustomed orderliness and method of their veryday life as they had known it in the bungalow in he south section of Chicago. They had bought a little ortable oven in a South Chicago hardware store. You ut it on the ground, stuffed it with wood, lighted it, nd in ten minutes it was red hot. Poli boiled potatoes, ried ham and eggs, even baked hot biscuits. Tony had igged up all sorts of ingenious devices—a cupboard, crews and bolts that dropped the back seat into a bed— hough they carried an auto tent. He was a wizard with tool kit. A contrivance at the back of the car dropped o make a dining table. Everything in the car pulled out,

shoved in, screwed, flapped, turned, disappeared, did
surprising flip-flops, became something it was not. It
was like a magic mammoth toy.

Three cooked meals a day at first; clean blankets;
washing; brushing; getting up at their accustomed hour;
sleeping at their accustomed hour. But slowly, gradually,
this old mode of living slipped from them. As they went
on, on, Poli sometimes would sing as they drove, in her
hoarse, low, rather eery voice, songs Tony had never
heard her sing even when she had been a bride and had
sung as she slammed about the kitchen of the old flat on
North Avenue.

"What's that you're singing?" he would ask. "So
crazy sounds."

"Huh?" She would act as though wakened out of a
sleep. "I didn't know at all was I singing. I don't know
I guess was a song old Grandma Zbado she would sing
all time when I was kid on Clybourn. Working around
she would sing all time to herself crazy songs like that."

Cars on the road, cars on the road, hundreds of them
streaming, skimming past fields, prairies, plains, mesas.
Cars like their own, filled with sunburned men whose
hands, on the wheel, were workgrimed; women with
faces reminiscent of old-country peasant stock. Cars
distorted with lumpy bundles, sacks, bales, bunches
like their own. Cars popping with children, swarthy or
tow-headed.

"Where you headin' f'r?" these would call to them
or they to these.

"West," was the vague answer, with a gesture toward
the setting sun. "I dunno. West."

They drove all day. At night the public camp grounds
of the Western towns were swarming with their kind.
The camp ground was usually a littered lot in a grove of
cottonwoods or willows. They streamed in at five, at
six, at seven, the dust-covered caravaners. Usually there
was a hut equipped with gas plates, and for five cents
you could cook your food over the gas flame. For another
five cents you got hot water. The women did bits of
washing. The men's faces gleamed dusky in the half
light. The women looked shapeless, grotesque, sometimes mysterious, witchlike. A new Romany band they
were, born of a modern invention, seeking cool lands in
summer, warm lands in winter.

"Is like old times," Poli said once to Tony.

"How old times?"

"In old country. How they used to go. On'y in
wagons."

"Yeh?" He did not know what she meant. Was
content. They were happy.

Sometimes Tony regarded her curiously. She became
more and more like the bold, careless, wild girl who had
caught his eye and held it that night in the pink dress
at Prudential Halk Crimpers no longer tortured her hair
at night. It streamed free, black, abundant. Her skin
was tanned the colour of leather. Instinctively she
seemed to know queer things—how to drink out of a
mountain brook, lying flat on her stomach and lipping
up the icy water. She was adept at building fires. Once
she called him her Velvet Georgie.

"Whaddyou mean, Georgie?" he asked humorously.
"Talkin' in your sleep?" (The comic movies.)

She was not talking in her sleep. "Oh, I dunno. I must of heard it somew'eres. Nickname."

The prim orderliness of their life gave way to rougher, more primitive habits. Sometimes they ate twice a day only, or munched a handful of something at noon as they drove. At night she would cook one dish in a black pot—a hot, savoury mess stewed in the kettle and spicy with chile, onions, tomatoes. This they ate with great draughts of hot coffee, revivifying, stimulating after a long day's drive. Then they would sleep deeply, dreamlessly, like tired animals.

As they drove, the golden road disappeared mile after mile, endlessly, into the rapacious maw of the little car. When Poli first beheld the mountains she gave a queer little savage cry and half stood up in the car, as though moved to leap from it.

Days became weeks. Their life became more primitive. Their high ambition was to find a spot where there were both water and shade at the end of the day.

"Is better as working, huh, Tony?"

"I betcha."

"We don't work no more, huh?"

"How you mean don't work no more, crazy, you! Starve to deat', huh?

"Starve not'ing. You said how that man back in La Junta, Colorado, he give you seven dollar a day for work in Santa Fé shops there. Always you could find job for little while, and save money, and then go on some more, riding."

"Yeh, riding! Riding where?"

"Anywheres. Where other people is always riding."

"Crazy, you! Crazy woman!"

She waxed sullen, silent, moody.

They approached Albuquerque, New Mexico, saw Indians for the first time. She became excited, garrulous. They must stop here. They must stop here. There was a fair in progress at the city's edge and near this they camped. Next morning when they awoke they found that they had been robbed. Tony's wallet was gone, filched neatly while he slept, though he had taken all the usual precautions to protect it. Frightened, bewildered, he went off to the heart of town to declare his loss, to communicate with Louie back in Chicago, thankful for the solid sum in the South Chicago bank.

"I guess we are through now, touring," he said grimly.

"Through! Why through? To California! We go to California, like we say."

"Naw. We going back home all right."

She protested frenziedly. "No! I don't go back! You see. I don't go."

He left her sulking in the tent. People were flocking to the fair grounds. The grounds were all astir. The bright western sun, the intense blue of the sky, the great white puffballs of cloud ballooning on the horizon, all promised a fine day. The sage-green mesa stretched away to the purple mountain peaks, snow-capped. He sighed as he drove into town. On a platform near the fair grandstand some acrobats were testing their apparatus for the day's early performance. In their tights the women, with their great thighs and torsos and hard muscular legs, looked grotesque as they went through with their writhings and squirmings with the illimitable mesa and the vast serene mountains as a background to shame them. They were like fat bugs under a cruel microscope.

He came back at noon with the assurance that there would be money for him in a day or two, telegraphed by Louie in Chicago. He felt relieved, almost happy, and yet vaguely regretful.

He came to their tent. The flap was open. Pinned to the outside was a sign printed crudely: "Gipsy Fortun Teler."

He stared, mouth ludicrously open. Then he lurched in, his big frame brushing the sides of the tent and shaking it. Half blinded by the glare of the sunshine from without, he could dimly discern two figures seated on camp chairs, close together. One, a woman unknown to him; the other almost equally strange. This one had one of his red cotton handkerchiefs knotted about her head, from which her black hair streamed to the waist. Around her neck were bright-coloured cheap Indian beads. Brass hoops dangled from her ears. Her eyes gleamed catlike in her swarthy face. Poli, reverted to type.

One syllable only, and a gesture. "Out!" he said to the unknown woman into whose palm Poli had been peering. This one gasped, snatched her hand away, fled through the opening into the safe outer sunshine, away from the terrifying man with the rolling eyeballs. At sight of him Poli, too, had cowered a little—but only a little. She rose, faced him, eyes and teeth and earrings and beads flashing.

"I make money. I make big money telling fortune so we can go some more."

"Take that rag off from your head. We pack up. We go home now. Crazy *tzigane*, you!"

Back, then, away from the western sun, their faces toward the east. Mountains faded into mesa, and mesa became plain, and plain became prairie, and prairie became field. Jog left; right on Galena Avenue. The Lincoln Highway. South Chicago. Home. The bungalow, set in the midst of the Illinois prairie, looking strangely populous now, and urban. Louie was there to meet them, and Pauline and Emmy, and a brood of children, and there was much clamour and coffee.

The strike? Well, Louie thought, them fools was about ready to give in an' call it a day and get back to the old job. Had a stummick full of it, he guessed, layin' around doing nothing. Papers said any day it'd be fixed an' the bosses would give'm the le's go sign. Well, pretty good to get home, huh? Little old Chicago looked pretty good to'm, huh?

Poli, at the kitchen sink, said nothing. The brood was off now, piling into the cars at the roadside and driving away, hands waving, children squalling. They stood on the front porch. Tony and Poli, looking out across the dull, drab Illinois prairie landscape to where the leaden clouds hung low so that sky and prairie seemed to be closing in all about them.

Poli, gazing, said nothing. Tony passed a brown hand over his stubble beard, scratched his grizzling head, spat. "Je's, it looks little!" he said.

Poli, gazing, said nothing. But a new hope welled in her.

OUR VERY BEST
PEOPLE

OUR VERY
BEST PEOPLE

Edna Ferber

OUR VERY BEST PEOPLE

IF RUTGER G. TUNE had waited two weeks longer to die he would have had to do a lot of explaining. And he always had hated explanations. They bored him. He died as he had lived, soldier of fortune that he was, with his spats on. Not only that, they were fawn spats, setting off a gray morning suit further enhanced by a flower in the buttonhole. There were few other—if any—fawn spats, gray morning suits, or beflowered buttonholes in Kansas City, Missouri, twenty years ago.

A plump, high-coloured, well-dressed figure of a middle-aged man, he had just passed debonairly through the gates of the Kansas City Union Station on his way to take the eastbound train, a deferential dusky porter ahead of him, when suddenly he crumpled, sank, and became a mere heap of haberdashery on the station platform. Confusion, crowds, telegrams. And the Tune twins, already motherless, were summoned home from Vassar to find themselves pretty much in the position of the Two Orphans of drama fame, so far as finances and future were concerned.

One week after the funeral: "But what did he *do* with it!" demanded Hilda Tune, the beauty. Her tone was perhaps excusably querulous considering that she and her sister Hannah now found themselves possessed of exactly nine hundred and twenty dollars each, the lawyers having just finished explaining,

"He didn't have it," replied Hannah, the plain twin, composedly.

"Didn't have it! What nonsense, Hannah. What did we live on all these years! Our education and clothes, and this huge house, and Father's wine and food and horses and . . ." Her voice trailed off. Then again, in helpless wrath, "What did we *live* on?"

"Bluff," said Hannah.

Even then, stricken though she was, Hilda had the good taste to be offended. "I wish you wouldn't use words like that, Hannah. And I do wish you wouldn't be any more vulgar than you can help."

Hannah was good-humoured enough about it, as always. "I'm not being a bit more vulgar than I can help. Besides, it's in the dictionary. Let's not quarrel now, Hilda. I simply meant that I don't think Father has had much money, really, in the last few years. I think he must have been worrying for quite a while about how he was going to explain things. He'd have had to explain in another week or two. And he knew it couldn't be done."

"But Mother left heaps. And there was all that stock in the packing company."

"Yes, but Father squandered heaps. The stock must have gone years ago."

"But it was ours! Lots of it was ours! Yours and mine."

Hannah smiled grimly. "You must have understood something of what Mr. Patterson and that other

lawyer meant when they said that Father had been
unwise in his handling of the money. He gambled,
among other things. So the money went, and the stocks
went, and this house is mortgaged right up to the
shingles. Father died owing practically everybody in
Kansas City from the First National Bank to the boy
who delivers the evening paper. We haven't any real
right to this precious nine hundred and twenty dollars
they've bestowed on us. . . . Well, if we've learned
anything practical at school, Hilda, my gal, now's a
grand chance to prove it."

An Eastern finishing school, followed by Vassar, had
rarely turned out a more unfinished product than
Hannah Tune, who was, she would explain to you, the
elder of the Tune twins. Hannah resembled her simple,
straightforward, plain-featured mother, who had been
the Kansas City heiress of the stockyards stock. Hilda
was undeniably her father's daughter—authentic off-
spring of Rutger G. Tune, of the Massachusetts Tunes,
who were born to be ancestors as some people are born
singers, writers, drunkards. A true Tune, posing for a
casual snapshot, always emerged looking like a portrait
by Sir Joshua Reynolds.

Rutger G. Tune, having bestowed upon the plain
Kansas City heiress his name, the charm of his occasional company, and the twin daughters, had considered
his obligations ended and had set about enjoying what
there was to enjoy in this mid-western town to which
he had come. Kansas City, though it sniggered at his
lemon-coloured spider phaëton with its two smart
trotters and flunkey seated up behind, really felt a

thrill of pride in the picture it all made as Tune, perched high on the fawn-cushioned box in his cream covert coat, his whip held at an angle of ninety, his hat just a little on one side, clipped briskly down Gilham Boulevard and whirled into The Paseo at an hour when the rest of Kansas City's adult male population was turning nickles into mickles as fast as it could. He practically represented the city's masculine leisure class.

From his lofty vantage he would greet the towns-people with that specious air of democracy peculiar to the born snob. "H'are you, Lindsey!.... 'Morning, Mrs. Horner!" His fine colour high, his full lips smiling.

"Get on to the hat!" giggled Kansas City, nudging its neighbour. "He's fixed up like one of those dining-room pictures—*you* know. English prints, they call 'em." Nevertheless, the town felt a vicarious thrill when a Tune horse won an Eastern race. The racing sheet would read, "Twin Girls. Rutger G. Tune, Owner." His favourite racing horse, bought at about the time of their birth, had been named in compliment to Hilda and Hannah.

It had been part of his snobbishness that he had sent the girls to Eastern schools in their very early teens. Also, when the Tunes travelled it was always in the East, or in Europe. They knew practically nothing of the vast country that stretched for thousands of miles west of Missouri to the Pacific. Mrs. Tune had loved her Middle West; had refused to live in the East, though her husband had urged it throughout her lifetime; and she had, during that lifetime and even after, made it financially difficult for her handsome husband to remain long away from the city whence her income had its source. The twins had once been taken to see the Colorado Rockies briefly and somewhat remotely, at Colorado Springs. Western railroad society was largely represented at the Antlers Hotel. Rutger G. Tune had not liked it. "A lot of brakemen," he said, "who have worked their way up through promotions to superintendencies; and their wives who have been waitresses, probably, in the Harvey station eating houses."

Mrs. Tune, though plain, had been a woman of spirit. She had spoken up at this. "My father used to say that those Western railroad brakemen and Harvey lunch-room waitresses were the future aristocracy of the West. Fine stock, he used to say, for foundation material. 'Pick out,' he said, 'almost any well-dressed, intelligent, prosperous-looking woman who is the wife of a successful ranch owner, Santa Fé railroad official, mining or oil man living within one thousand miles of the Mojave desert, and ask her if she was born in the West. She'll answer, 'Oh, no. I'm from Iowa' (or maybe Wisconsin, or Michigan, or Kansas, or even Ohio). 'I used to be a Harvey girl.' Pa always said they were a fine lot, those Harvey waitresses. Smart, independent. Had come West because they wanted to see the country, probably, and were tired of some kind of tyranny in the East. Pioneer stuff, Pa said. I used to like to hear him when he said that New England had its Lowells and Cabots and Lodges, and the South its Van Revels and Colonel Carters and its F. F. V.'s; but that out in Arizona and Texas and Colorado and New Mexico it was the children of the ranchers and railroad men and the ex-Harvey girls who would form the future back-bone of——"

"Well," interrupted Rutger G. Tune, his moustache coming up under his nose, "I prefer my hired girls in the kitchen, not the parlour."

The Harvey system, with its chain of lunch rooms and dining rooms stretching across a continent from Chicago through the very desert itself and beyond, to California, was the boast of any true Westerner. Mrs. Tune's pride in it was incomprehensible to her Eastern-born husband. "Beastly idea, anyway," he said, "having to get off a train for your meals, like that. And those cow towns!"

"We like it," said Mrs. Tune, spiritedly.

"We?"

"We Westerners. And I noticed that you like the quail pretty well that they served you at the station of that cow town called Newton. You'd have paid ten dollars a portion for it in New York—and then it wouldn't have been fresh."

Still, they did not travel West again. But she loved it to the day she died.

At school the twins, Hilda and Hannah, had been known respectively as Tune and Cartoon. For Nature, in her most prankish mood, having fashioned these two in like mould, yet had so slightly, so deftly, so fiendishly over-emphasized in Hannah that which was perfection in Hilda that perfection became grotesquerie—or almost that. It was only when they were together that the difference was strongly marked. People—strangers—

seeing the two for the first time had a way of turning
from the flawless purity of Hilda's contour to the exaggerated line that was Hannah's, and then blinking a
little as though to rid themselves of an absurd optical
illusion. It was as though Nature, having wrought
this perfect thing, had said, pettishly, "What! You
expect me to achieve this miracle a second time! No!
Here, I'll make a rough copy of it. But a masterpiece is a
masterpiece. One doesn't repeat."

Hence Tune and Cartoon. Where Hilda's nose was
the most exquisite example of that ordinarily vulgar
feature, straight, fine-pored, delicately fluted at the
nostrils, Hannah's, being the minutest fraction of an
inch longer, was just too long; and the fluting, being a
trifle wider, gave her countenance that rather com-
bative look so trying to the beholder. Where Hilda's
cheek bones were just high enough to give her face its
delicately heart-shaped outline and her eyes that little
shadowed look of fatigue which men find so fascinating,
Hannah's cheek bones were broader, flatter, so that she
had a somewhat Slavic cast. Still, if it had not been for
Hilda's flawless beauty always there to mock her,
Hannah might have been considered an average-looking
girl, which she really was: healthy, high-spirited,
wholesome. For that matter, there were those who
might have thought Hilda's lips a shade too thin, just
as others thought Hannah's mouth too large. That
generous mouth of Hannah Tune's was the index of her
character. It explained why she could be honestly proud
and pleased when people exclaimed about her sister's
loveliness. It made it possible for Hannah to say, as she

watched the exquisite Hilda march across the greensward at the head of the historic Daisy Chain (the very day of the tragic telegram), that if the college had instituted a Poison Ivy Chain she, Hannah, would have been a prominent entrant.

People who knew them well were aware that the difference between the twins was more than a surface one. It went deep, deep into their characters. It cropped out in all sorts of ways. You saw it in the accumulated dust of days in the seeming dainty Hilda's hairbrush; in the condition of her bureau drawers; in the frequency with which she forgot to pay back money she had borrowed from Hannah; in her unfailing emphasis on the Tune side of her ancestry, ignoring quite the distaff or Packing House side; her refusal to mingle with any but those whom she considered the most desirable type of girl at college. Her tone, in speaking of the undesirables, was startlingly like that of Rutger G. Tune when he had discussed the brakemen and Harvey waitresses years before. Hannah's familiar at college, on the other hand, had been a girl from Galena, Illinois, who had got a scholarship and was working her way through. Hannah's old red sweater and her careless tam were likely to give you no hint of the fastidious freshness of the garments worn beneath—the beribboned corset cover, the white embroidery petticoats, the lace-trimmed umbrella drawers of the period. Finally, this difference in face and character had been less pronounced when they were children; became daily more noticeable as they grew older.

It had been June when Rutger G. Tune caused the little flurry in the Union Station and the great upheaval in the lives of his motherless twin daughters. In July the twins were to leave the big Tune house perched high on the hill that commanded such a sweeping and unobstructed Missouri view of nothing in particular.

"Father had it built up here," Hannah observed, a little grimly, perhaps, but without bitterness, "not because anything could be seen here from the top of the hill, but because everybody could see the house from the bottom of it. That's what our life has been, really, in the last ten years. A magnificent view of nothing at all."

The two had soberly been discussing that baffling problem known as Ways and Means. Of Ways they had few. Of Means they had practically nothing.

"There's only one thing to do, of course," Hilda said; "that is, to get away from here. And there's only one place to go, and that's East. Our friends there know Father's dead, but they don't know how completely smashed we are. I shan't tell them until I have to. We both have enough invitations to last through the summer, if we manage properly. The Allisters at Bar Harbor in July, and Isabel Kane's the first two weeks in August in the Adirondacks, and we might even manage Newport if we went about it properly and used a little——"

"And then what?" interrupted Hannah, bluntly.

"I don't know. But, at any rate, we'd have made a

move in the right direction. Our friends in the East are numbered among the very best people. Those are the contacts we'll have to keep up."

"On nine hundred and twenty dollars per lifetime?"

"Yes. Why not! Until something turns up. And it will, with those people back of us. There's something picturesque about being twins. It's considered chic. And orphan twins, too."

"And penniless orphan twins makes it quite perfect, I suppose."

"All right, then. Suppose you suggest something better."

Hannah, for the moment, looked as nearly helpless as Hannah could, being handicapped by her height, her serenity of brow, and her aura of superb health. "I honestly haven't anything better to suggest, Hilda. I only know I can't go East with you and live on our very best people and be a chic twin."

"What are you going to do, then? What are you going to do? Stay here in Kansas City! Patronized by these people! What'll you live on? Really, Hannah, sometimes I think you're utterly——"

"I could teach school."

"Teach school!" Hilda echoed weakly. "You mean a girls' school somewhere in the East? But what? Your French isn't very good, and you know your English is—well, it's pure Kansas City. Your music is just passable. You hate history."

"Oh, I mean a school here somewhere in Kansas, maybe. A country school. It doesn't pay much, but it's a living, for the present at least. Besides, I like the West.

You know that. I always have. A country school—and a
horse to ride, maybe, Saturdays and Sundays. I'd like it."

"Hannah Tune, you must be crazy! A country school!
A horse on Saturday!"

"And Sunday," put in Hannah, a trifle maliciously—
for Hannah. Suddenly she became tremendously serious.
Her fine brow bore down upon Hilda, silencing her.
"Look here, Hilda Tune. There's no use pretending
we're not in a mess. We are. But we always have been.
We simply didn't know it, that's all. But Father knew
it, and shut his eyes to it, and pretended that something
would turn up. Well, it didn't. Mercifully, he died before
he had to do any explaining. Now, I'm not going on
where he left off. I'm sick of pretending. I'm the plain
Tune twin, with nine hundred and twenty dollars between me and whatever happens to you when your
money's all gone. It's no use my trying to play the
beautiful adventuress. I'm not equipped for it in face or
temperament. It's July, and pretty late, but I'm going
to try to get a school job by September, somewhere."

A sort of glaze crept over Hilda's beautiful face,
hardening it. "All right, then. Be a schoolma'am. But
don't expect me to stay here with you. Sometimes,
Hannah, I think there isn't a drop of Tune blood in
you."

Hannah seemed to consider this a compliment. "I
know it. After all these years of pruning and snipping
here I am, just bristling all over with Kansas. I guess
there's no help for it."

Hilda, looking lovely and fragile in black, went to the
Allisters at Bar Harbor. Hannah had not yet secured a

school, but there were rumours of one to be had in
Eldorado, Kansas. "Oh, my goodness!" Hilda had
said, when she heard of it. At the last minute Hannah
had stuffed five hundred of her own nine hundred and
twenty into Hilda's bag. "I won't need it," she said,
above Hilda's faint protests. "I'll be earning money
soon. And you'll want it pretty badly if you're going to
make any kind of showing in the among-those-present
column in the Newport society news. Linsey-woolsey,
whatever that is, will be all I'll need in Eldorado."

By the first of August Hannah was told the Eldorado
school was hers. She wrote Hilda the news, jubilantly.
Hilda was in the Adirondacks, according to schedule.
Hannah got ready her linsey-woolseys, including the old
red sweater of college skating days. In the middle of
August Hannah was notified that Eldorado's last year's
teacher was returning after all; and that here was one
month's salary, and that it was hoped Miss Tune had
been put to no inconvenience.

Miss Tune was not only inconvenienced but indignant, and a little frightened. Her first impulse was to
telegraph Hilda; so she didn't. The Tune twins had been
brought up on telegrams. Rutger G. Tune had hated
letter-writing. At this critical moment a telegram from
Hilda (her father's daughter) said that she had a chance
to go abroad in October with Mrs. Courtney Paige, as a
sort of pet pampered companion. And what did Hannah
think about it? Hannah, feeling suddenly alone in the
world, and terribly twinless, answered: "It sounds
heavenly. You must go." Then she began to read the
want ad columns of the Kansas City *Star*.

M-m-m-m-m-m—clerks wanted. Experienced. . . . Binders wanted. What was a binder? Hannah wondered. And what did they bind? . . . Ladies to solicit orders for marvellous new patent contrivance warranted to revolutionize housework. On commission only. . . . Waitresses wanted—oh, my goodness!—what was there for her to do! Wait a minute! . . . waitresses wanted for Harvey hotel dining rooms and lunch rooms in Colorado, New Mexico, Arizona, and California. Apply Employment Department, Union Station, Room 15.

Something came creeping back into Hannah's consciousness like the fragments of a song once heard and long forgotten . . . "fine stock . . . pioneer stuff . . . Harvey waitresses . . . future aristocracy . . ."

Hannah had been a very little girl when her mother, with that look of high pride and honest indignation, had delivered herself of that speech. But it came back to her now, as did the sneer on her father's face. Colorado—New Mexico—Arizona—California! Hannah took a long breath, exhaled it, and applied Employment Department, Union Station, Room 15.

She had a little sick feeling at the pit of her stomach, and her knees seemed strangely fluid; but there was a picture of the Grand Cañon on the wall of the little waiting room, and a map whose black lines went bounding across mountains and deserts and plains and mesas in a way to take your breath away. Hannah regarded these, and they gave her courage and even a feeling of exaltation which always came to her, strangely enough, when she caught a remote hint of that which lay Pacificward from Missouri. A little soaring sensation. A feeling of freedom. If she had had wings she would have flapped them now.

There were five other girls in the anteroom. One of them had a foreign look—Polish or Bohemian, Hannah thought. Two, evidently friends, had entered together exhaling a stench of cheap perfume. Hannah thought they didn't look exactly pioneer material or future aristocrats. A fourth was a pale quiet girl who appeared listless and limp. "She's going out for her health," Hannah decided. "Arizona, probably, if they'll take her." The fifth girl resembled Hannah's Vassar chum from Galena, Illinois. Hannah found herself smiling at this girl, companionably. The girl smiled back at her. Encouraged thus, Hannah moved to a chair next to her. "Are you—have you ever—are you going out West as a Harvey girl?"

"Yes—to stay this time, I hope."

"Oh, you've been before?"

"Two years ago. But only for the summer. I'm a school teacher. I took a Harvey job two summers ago because I thought it would be fun, kind of; and a cheap way to see something of the West. I'm from Albia, Iowa. You ought to have heard my folks when I said I was going as a waitress. They didn't know."

"And now you're going to stay?"

"Long as I want to, anyway. I'm lucky. They're sending me to the Cañon." Then, as Hannah looked blank—"Oh, I guess you don't know about the different stations. You see, all the girls are crazy to go to the hotels at the Grand Cañon, or Albuquerque, or big places like that. We call them heaven. Now, Needles,

California, and Rincon, New Mexico, are purgatory. We say that's where bad girls go for punishment. Needles is two hundred miles from the Mojave desert, in a sort of pocket. And hot! Phew! When it's a hundred and twenty-five there they think it's getting on toward summer."

Hannah looked a little worried. "Do you think a new girl——"

The other shook her head emphatically. "Some. But not you." Her glance encompassed Hannah's face, her clothes, her manner. "Gracious, no! You look like a Cañon girl, or Albuquerque, except that perhaps you'll lose out because you're too pretty."

Hannah stared, smiled. "Me!"

"You know, don't you, that Harvey's never hire girls that are awfully pretty. They found they couldn't keep them out West. They just melted away into marriage with some rancher or railroad man or mining——"

"Then it's true!"

But the other girl misunderstood. "Oh, my yes. They like to hire them neat, plain, and sensible. They're very strict, you know. You've got to behave just so during hours—and after hours, for that matter. In before twelve——" She broke off suddenly as the door to the inner office opened. She was next in the list of waiting applicants. "See you later. Wish me luck!"— over her shoulder.

Hannah never saw her again. Two days later Hannah Tune, daughter of the late Rutger G. Tune of the Massachusetts Tunes, to whom the Signers of the Declaration of Independence were mere upstarts, was

on her way to San Querto, New Mexico, with a Harvey
Santa Fé railroad pass in her handbag. She was enjoying
herself immensely, though the ride was hot, dusty, and
seemingly endless. Every now and then she went into
the washroom and scraped prairie dust off her clothes
and face and railroad cinders out of her hair. Then she
washed for the sake of the relief the cool wet towel gave
against her hot cheeks, and went back to her seat to
resume her staring out of the window. Prairie, plain,
corn, corn, corn, corn—hundreds of miles of it, an
unmarine ocean, billowing away and away to the
horizon. And, like the ocean, it makes the beholder
content or restless. Hannah felt soothed, relaxed,
satisfied.

With her Sante Fé pass was an identification card
entitling her to meals free of charge at all stops where
meals were regularly scheduled. At these stations along
the way passengers were notified that they would have
half an hour for lunch. They swarmed out of the coaches
like ants from a disturbed ant hill. The sound of a deep-
throated brass gong greeted them as they flocked
toward the dining and lunch rooms. Hannah soon
discovered that she preferred the rush and scramble
of the lunch rooms to the more dignified and orderly
ceremony of the dining room. Her first meal in the
dining room at Hutchinson, Kansas, had been of im-
mense interest to her, flavoured with almost hysterical
amusement. She had never imagined anything like it.
A hundred, or even two hundred passengers were fed
here in half an hour. The meal marched as inevitably,
as irresistibly as death itself. Each table seated eight.

The first course lay smoking before you as you seated yourself. With that scant half hour snapping at their heels the passengers settled grimly, determinedly, to this business of consuming their dollar's worth. It was a huge meal, hot, savoury, appetizing. But the dining hundreds made a ghastly ceremony of it. Not a murmur of conversation; eyes on their plates. They were devastating, thorough. No sounds but the clink of cutlery against china, the low voices of the white starched waitresses murmuring a chant of "Teacoffeemilk? Teacoffeemilk? Teacoffeemilk?" Controlling, soothing this strange company, as unconvivial as the elfin bowlers in Rip Van Winkle's mountain retreat, walked the Harvey hotel manager, bland, watchful, weaving in and out among the tables, hands behind his back. And as he walked he intoned: "Pas-sen-gers on Number Nine have *thirty minutes* for dinner. Take—your—time!" Fifteen minutes later, again as before: "Pas-sen-gers on Number Nine still have *fifteen* minutes for dinner. Take—your—time!" Gobble gobble. Clink clink. Gulp gulp. Munch munch. Soup, meat, vegetables, salad, olives, iced tea, dessert. "Pas-sen-gers on Number Nine still have *five minutes*——" They swept out like a horde of locusts, leaving a ravaged dining room.

No, Hannah decided, the dining room was not for her. She would eat in the lunch room where ham and eggs, ordered one minute, appeared miraculously before you the next; where hovered the scent of coffee; where blood-red half moons of watermelon glowed at you from behind glass; where you sat perched on a revolving stool before a white slab of counter, with infinitesimal cream pitchers and little butter chips and glasses of ice water spinning and sliding all about you. Hannah became less and less a Tune; more and more the daughter of her plain, democratic, high-spirited mother.

This trip had all the flavour of a stolen holiday, for the truth of it is that, at the last moment, she had not had the courage to tell her plans to Hilda. She lacked the courage to write to Hilda, there in the Adirondacks at the Kanes' elaborately rustic lodge, "I am going West to be a Harvey hired girl." Instead, she had given Hilda to understand that her mission at San Querto was to teach school. She dilated on it, in her guilt, and made it sound quite picturesque and charming. Much nicer, she said, than the Eldorado school, about which she had decided adversely.

Hannah had been in San Querto almost ten days before her twin's reply reached her. "I suppose," wrote Hilda, among other things, "you'll be the pretty Western school teacher of the movies, rescued from Indians by a rancher in chaps and frijoles, or whatever it is they wear, and marry him, and live happily ever after. Can you possibly spare me some money, Cartoon dear?"

Hannah, in her black uniform and white apron, read the letter as she stood behind the counter in a quiet hour at the San Querto station lunch room. She had just emerged from the bewilderment, shock, and chaos of the past ten days. A certain accustomed serenity again sat on her brow. In those ten days she had learned much, suffered much, wept much, slept little. She had learned and suffered in the Harvey lunch room; wept and lain awake in the little bare, clean, whitewashed bedroom on the top floor of the Sante Fé station, with the engines puffing, hissing, snorting, clanging in her racked head; grinding, it seemed, over her very knees. And yet so miraculously do we adjust ourselves to environment (if we are Hannahs) that now the white-tiled lunch room seemed a zestful cheery place, and the little white-walled bedroom a snug refuge where she could be alone. The trains, after a fortnight, bothered her no more than does the chirping of birds the country dweller.

Now she read her letter in a quiet moment between trains, seated on a little stool behind the horseshoe of counter. It had just been handed her by the hotel manager. "Letter from home?" asked Louise, the red-haired girl.

"From my twin sister."

"Twins! Don't say! Do you look just alike?"

"Oh, no," Hannah said, rather absently, dipping into her letter again. "Not a bit. My sister's a beauty."

Louise looked at her sharply as she sat there in her neat black and white, her hair done in the smooth simple fashion that the Harvey rules decreed, her throat rising so firm and white from the flat collar that finished the neckline of her blouse. "Well, you're no eyesore!" she exclaimed.

Hannah had smiled quietly. "You ought to see Hilda."

She sent Hilda two hundred dollars of the tiny sum that now remained of her original nine hundred and twenty.

By the end of the month Hanna had learned so much that it seemed to her as if, until now, she had merely been marking time. She had learned things pleasant and disagreeable; interesting and dull; exhilarating and depressing. She learned to call scheduled trains by their names, as if they were individuals—Number Nine— Number Thirteen—Number Five. Number Eight's due in from the West. There's Number Eleven from the East. She learned to remember six orders taken at one time in the rush of the crowd just off a waiting train. She learned to keep her head when under a fire of orders volleyed at her like hail.

"Ham 'n' eggs!"

"Apple pie! Glass milk!"

"Coffee!"

"Cheese on rye!"

"Liver 'n' onions!"

Short. Sharp. Relentless. Inescapable, Stinging.

She learned that San Querto itself, though an important Santa Fé railroad division point, was an ugly little Mexican town, squatting flat on the mesa, its new houses staring and unlovely, its Old Town, where the Mexicans lived, squalid and unpicturesque. Its roads were mud wallows, its main street sordid, its Mexicans lazy, dirty, and thieving. Yet there was the Western mountain air, and there was the Western sky, and there, beyond the town, were the Spanish Peaks, those mysterious purple-black twin mountains rising abruptly, without warning, magically, from the flat mesa itself. They were, Hannah thought, like no other mountain peaks in the world. They thrilled her, bewitched her. When first they had loomed up before her as she gazed out of her train window she had given a little cry and had

sat forward in her seat, staring. There stretched the
sage-green mesa, for miles. Not a foothill. Not even a
hillock. Then, suddenly, without preparation, rising
out of this flat plateau and soaring straight up to snow,
loomed the purple Spanish Peaks against the sunset sky.
The tears had come to Hannah's eyes. She felt as if she
had come home.

Now she had learned to look at them the first thing
in the morning; to peer into the darkness in their
direction the last thing at night. She learned to wash
and iron her own shirtwaists. She learned to ride a
Western horse on mountain roads. She learned to work
"nights one week, days one week," without feeling
sleepy during night-work week. She learned that cowboys, though picturesque, do not change their shirts
as often as they might. She learned those feats of
legerdemain which all waitresses acquire through experience—a certain swing of the ketchup bottle—a
juggling of hot coffee cups—a whisk of the towel.

And she learned to watch for the entrance of Dan
Yard. Dan Yard was substitute brakeman on a branch-
line freight train running into San Querto four nights
a week. A substitute brakeman on a branch-line freight
train is the lowest possible position in the railroad world.

She had first seen him in the second week of her coming to San Querto. She was working nights, that week.
He had come off his train at 2 A. M., and had dropped
into the lunch room after washing up, as was the custom
of brakemen, engineers, and conductors at the end of
a run, for a cup of coffee and a sandwich, or a couple
of doughnuts. It was against rules for Harvey girls to

carry on social conversation with lunch-counter patrons. No pretense of swishing imaginary crumbs off the slab while exchanging flirtatious pleasantries with the willing cowboys, ranchmen, or railroad men was allowed here. A greeting, yes. An amiable word or two. But that was all. Yet Hannah noticed a little intangible change come over the two girls on duty with her that night as Dan Yard swung open the screen door and, entering, threw one leg over a stool at the counter, pushed back his cap, and smiled. His smile was not the fictional smile of rare sweetness, lighting up his whole face. It was a schoolboy grin, engaging, but somewhat tough.

"Any raspberries?" inquired Dan of the girl at whose station he was seated.

"Yes."

"Well, I don't want any."

"Thought you didn't." Having taken her part in this brilliant dialogue which was evidently a formula, she set before him a cup of smoking coffee and his plate of doughnuts. Hannah, by now, was hardened to seeing monstrous food consumed at unseemly hours. Half hidden by the nickel coffee urn she turned to look at him. He dumped three generous spoonfuls of sugar into his cup, emptied the contents of his cream pitcher, stirred the mixture and took a great swallow of the scalding, revivifying liquid. The size of that great gulp brought his head up and back so that he found himself staring at Hannah over the rim of his inverted cup. Hannah's gaze met his. *Ting!* went something like a bell inside her.

She saw a slim, hard, rather pugnacious-looking young

Irishman of perhaps twenty-four or five. Freckled. His eyes were wide apart, clear, and singularly bright. She thought she had never seen anyone so wide awake at 2 A. M. He evidently had just washed with strong soap and slicked his hair after coming in off his run. His head was damp where the pocket comb had tidied it. Later Hannah learned that he was bowlegged and some three inches shorter than she. All their married life (for she married Dan Yard) she tried not to let him feel this difference in their height; did her hair flat and wore lowheeled shoes, for she loved him terribly and he was a sensitive and somewhat vain Irishman, as all good Irishmen are.

What Dan Yard saw of Hannah over the rim of his upturned coffee cup she never quite knew. He never seemed able to put it into coherent words. He would begin, when she asked him: "I said to myself, 'There she is!' like that. 'There's Mrs. Dan Yard.' I felt all the blood up in my head, fit to smother me."

"It was the hot coffee."

"It was hot love," said Dan, being the reverse of mincing.

He had finished his coffee that night, had reached for his glass of ice water, swallowed it in one long draught, sliding one piece of conveniently sized ice into his mouth along with the fluid, and had walked out, crunching the ice between his strong yellow teeth.

"Why!" said the girl who had waited on him. "Look! Dan Yard never touched his doughnuts at all."

For six weeks Hannah withstood him. In those six weeks she learned much about Dan Yard. He came from a family of railroad workers. When he talked of this it was as though he were descended from a long line of aristocrats. His father had been Engine Man John Yard, killed in the wreck at Algodones in 1899. His brother was an engineer on the Burlington. His uncle was an engineer on the Santa Fé. Another uncle killed acting as yardmaster at La Junta. Two cousins were brakemen. Another a conductor. His family tree, and proud of it. He had almost gone through high school. Quit, his third year, because he had to go to work. By next January he would have his job as regular brakeman on the main line. Then they could be married.

"No!" said Hannah, trying to laugh. Terribly frightened, yet with a certain crazy feeling of warmth and happiness suffusing her whole being. Then "No," faintly, his eyes on hers and her own closing flutteringly as she felt his strong, hard, oil-grimed hand on her arm.

Hilda was in Europe. In January Hannah wrote her, fearfully yet boldly; and certainly baldly. "I am going to be married." They had been married some weeks before Hilda's reply reached them. "I hope he's one of those millionaire ranchers or oil kings that seem to grow exclusively out there in the West where men are men, or whatever it is the poem says." The hot tears of resentment and indignation came to Hannah's eyes. She spent hard-earned dollars to cable her answer, unthriftily worded:

"He's a king, all right, but not the kind you mean. Dan's a brakeman on the Santa Fé railroad."

A cable from Hilda: "You must be insane cable if joke."

Hannah replied, tersely, "No joke."

Silence. Silence that lasted twenty years.

They went housekeeping in one of the ugly little San Querto houses and became part of the little bare railroad town where caste lines were drawn as definitely as in Mayfair. Brakemen's wives were beneath freight-train conductors' wives in the social scale. Station masters' wives patronized conductors' wives. The wife of a division superintendent queened it over the wives of both station masters and passenger train conductors. As for the wife of a district superintendent! Royalty.

Hannah busied herself in the little house with its mission furniture and its Navajo rugs, but while Dan was gone she found time heavy on her hands, now that she had left the lunch room. She decided to learn to be a telegrapher, acquired this with amazing speed and was telegrapher at San Querto for two years, until her first child was born. They had two boys. Always there was with her that little fear ever present in the heart of the railroad worker's wife.

"Dan, I wish you'd stop railroading."

"Stop! What for?"

"I'm afraid you'll get k—hurt."

"Me! Naw! I won't get killed."

"They did."

"Not me."

The sound of the trains striding and elbowing their way in and out of this little railroad town, out to the prairies and mountains beyond, no longer disturbed her as mere noise. But she used to lie awake, always, on the nights when he was out on his run—wide awake, listening, until she heard the whistle of Number 7. Dan's train. Dangerous work, braking. She knew that. They made him freight-train conductor one year later. Not so dangerous and better pay. A step up the ladder. By the time she had got accustomed to her duties as telegrapher in the little station at San Querto he was promoted to yard master at that point. Dangerous again. Sitting in the little bay window of the shabby red brick station, her subconscious ear intent on the click of the keys, she would watch for him. It was his duty to shunt freight, direct the tangle of loaded and unloaded cars, see that they got in and out of the spider web of tracks, on their way East or West. When she saw the small wiry bowlegged figure crossing the tracks toward the station she would go to meet him, the old red sweater buttoned up tight about her full firm figure. It seemed to her that all her married life she was watching for that little wiry bowlegged figure from some window or other, all the way from the dilapidated station at San Querto to the window of the great Spanish hacienda that they built in 1920, within magnificent view of the Spanish Peaks. He never failed to appear just before fear had got its icy fingers on her heart. And she never let him know that she had been fearful.

The rise of Dan Yard is history in the annals of the Santa Fé road. They tell it as a sort of saga. Yet it all seemed natural enough in the actual happening. From brakeman to freight-train conductor; conductor to yard master; yard master to station master at San Querto. Hannah with him all the time, toning down his roughness ("tuning him down," she called it); saying, quietly, "Now, Dan," when he became too coltish. He liked a pretty face and a trim figure, and she knew it, and kept her figure trim, for she knew that to hold an Irishman you must be vigilant and wary. He was the kind of husband who breaks out occasionally into playful tousling of hair and pinching of cheeks and bruising squeezes of shoulder. When he got too rough—"Now, Dan," with fine dignity and composure. He would subside. But she enjoyed it, nevertheless. Just enough Tune in her to keep him impressed. Plenty of her spirited mother to hold him.

At thirty he became an "office man"; clerk to the division superintendent at San Querto. At thirty-three he was Division Superintendent. Hannah, if she cared to, could now queen it over the conductors' wives. For the Division Superintendent has a private car, if you please. Not a very good private car, it is true. An old passenger coach, usually, carefully gutted out and made over, fitted with compartments and finished in the old red wood and gimcracky scrollwork of a past era in railroad decoration. But a private car, nevertheless. They could use it to run to Omaha or to Kansas City, if they wanted to. Hannah Yard could take a carload of conductors' wives to the opera, if opera there happened to be within a distance of five hundred miles. But she never did.

From Division Superintendent he was promoted to District Superintendent. No trifling about it now. Dan Yard was an important man in the road. They say his wife had a lot to do with it. A smart woman, Mrs. Yard. And handsome isn't the name for it. They say she was

the daughter of Rutger G. Tune. Don't you remember?
Did you never hear of old Tune of Kansas City! Yeh.
Used to be a big bug and a sport. Went through his
wife's millions and died pretty shady. Well, nothing
shady about this Mrs. Yard. And Dan! Say, he'll be
General Manager yet. Watch him.

From District Superintendent to Assistant General
Superintendent. Then, inevitably, General Superintendent. There is, after that, only one step; but it is a mo-
mentous step; a seven-league stride. It is the unrealized
dream of every railroad official. It is not only the Chair
at His Right Hand. It is The Right Hand. General
Manager.

Dan Yard, at forty-six, was General Manager of the
Santa Fé road. The Yards' private car now was a thing
of rosewood and silken hangings and finest steel. They
were Royalty. Yet, twenty years later, if you happened
to be a guest in this private movable palace of theirs,
and if, peering out of the window in the darkness you
asked, "Where are we now, I wonder? What's this place
we're coming to?" Hannah Yard could close her eyes
and, listening intently a moment, say, "We're just
coming into Trinidad. I can tell by the bump of the
wheels over the rails. I was here when Dan laid out these
yards."

During these twenty years she had thought of Hilda
thousands of times, and sadly. She took the New York
Times as soon as they could afford it, in the hope of
seeing Hilda's name mentioned in the society columns,
perhaps. She wrote her, often. Her letters were un-
answered. When she placed a return address on these

letters they came back rubber-stamped, "Not at address given." Though Dan's position took him frequently to New York Hannah rarely accompanied him. She dreaded it, somehow. Once she had tried to trace Hilda there, but had not succeeded. She thought of a detective agency, but shrank from the idea. After all, Hilda had not wanted her; Hilda had deserted her, ridiculed her just when she needed her love most. She seldom spoke to Dan of Hilda; as the years went on Hilda's name was never mentioned. The two boys were at college—the elder at a school of engineering ("Like his pa," laughed Dan Yard); the other at an agricultural school. He wanted to be a rancher, and raise stock and alfalfa and oranges and sugar beets and cantaloupes.

"All on one ranch!" laughed his mother. "That isn't a ranch. That's a paradise."

The Yard place, a great glowing creamy Spanish pile situated in the valley, but on a slight rise, and almost in the shadow of the purple and mysterious Spanish Peaks, was known throughout the West. You were likely to find as guests there anyone from the President of the United States to a flock of Harvey waitresses on a ten-days' vacation. A Goya over the fireplace in the living room; a gorgeous old vestment of brocade and ancient velvet thrown over this screen bought in Granada. "Come on along to New York with me," said Dan Yard, in tousling mood. "Come on, old girl. Do you good. They sent me a catalogue of that Spanish stuff to be sold at Barrios'. There's one old tapestry velvet that sounds like the thing you want for that balcony railing, exactly. Come on. Let's take a look at it, anyway."

The General Manager's private car, summoned casually, like an automobile. Thousands of miles, over mountain passes, mesas, plains, prairies, cornfields. Omaha, Chicago, New York.

"I wired Barrios," said Dan, at breakfast in New York, "and he just called up to say he was sending some stuff over here to the hotel. I thought, as long as your head didn't feel so good this morning——"

A lean, wiry, pugnacious bowlegged little Irishman, looking, in spite of graying hair and his carefully tailored suit and the dignity of his office, incredibly like the tough young brakeman of the San Querto lunch room twenty years ago.

Like a cue in a play then, the telephone rang. Barrios' representative calling. And "Oh, dear!" said Hannah, glancing down at a foamy but informal negligee. "You talk to him for a minute, Dan, I'll do my hair and get into something. Don't let him sell you anything till I—you remember that terrible table you——"

As she dressed hurriedly she could hear him in the adjoining room.

"Well, say, that's pretty. . . . No, I don't like that one. . . . I don't know, I just don't like it. It doesn't look Spanish to me. My wife knows. She'll be in in a minute. She's . . . she may like it. . . . It don't look to me . . ."

A man's voice in low protest; then a woman's voice, high, hard, nervous, icy. "Not authentically Spanish! There are only two other pieces like it in the world. The other two were sold yesterday to a family representing our very best people. You will like it, I know, if you will just live with it a while. . . ."

Hannah, at her dressing table, stood up, clutching her dressing gown to her breast. She whirled to face her husband who had just come in. He was grinning. He dropped his voice to a rasping whisper. He even tiptoed, in some absurd delusion of increased secrecy.

"Say, Hannah, there's three of 'em sent up with the stuff from Barrios! A regular troupe. A kid to carry the bundles, and a young Spanish feller, and he's got on a lavender shirt and perfume, so help me God. But listen. Don't get mad at me, Hannah, when you see her—the woman—say—she looks enough like you, in a kind of an awful way, to be a cartoon of you. By golly, she does! A kind of snaky dress, and red stuff on her mouth, and talks about our best people . . ."

A sob of premonition shook Hannah Yard as she ran past her husband and into the next room to face the woman sent up from Barrios'.

PERFECTLY
INDEPENDENT

PERFECTLY
INDEPENDENT

Edna Ferber

PERFECTLY INDEPENDENT

MRS. HANAUER and Mrs. Grimm were perfectly independent. Frequently they reminded one another of the fact, and always with pride. They boasted of it to their friends. In hoity-toity moments Mrs. Hanauer said to her daughter and son-in-law (as did Mrs. Grimm to her son and daughter-in-law), "You don't have to look after me. Nobody has to bother about me. I'm perfectly independent."

This precious independence was not the only tie that bound these two in friendship. True, they were sufficiently unlike to prevent boredom. But their lives held much in common. Both were widows. Each dwelt alone, comfortably, occupying two rooms and bath in an expensive family hotel overlooking (to quote the ad) Central Park. In years both could see the sixties receding as the seventies loomed near. They enjoyed mah jong and bridge, commenting on each other's play with an insulting frankness that, in a professional game of chance, could have been wiped out only with blood. Each used the other as a safety valve. Alternately Mrs. Hanauer bragged and complained to Mrs. Grimm of her daughter and son-in-law. Mrs. Grimm's son and daughter-in-law came in for the same treatment.

In moments of triumph: "You'd think they couldn't do anything without me. It's Mother, what do you think

of this, and, Mother, what do you think of that? . . .
I told them they didn't want an old woman like me
along. But they said, 'All right. If you don't go, then we
won't.' . . . Ed sent me two tickets for the matinée. I
just happened to say I would like to see that Leonore
Ulric. It's got so I can't even mention a thing. The next
minute I have it. . . ." "Bernice brought me these handkerchiefs from Atlantic City. If I've got one I've got a
hundred. I said, 'Can't you and Jo even go away over
the week-end without thinking you have to bring me
something!' She said, 'Why, Mother, it isn't that we
think we have to. We love to.' They spoil me. Honestly,
you'd think I was . . ."

In other moments: "I told them! If I don't tell them
the truth, who will! I said I'd like to know what young
married people are thinking of nowadays. I'm not a
person to make trouble between husband and wife.
And Stella can't say that I ever said a word to turn Ed
against her. I hope I'm too modern a mother-in-law
for that. But I said to Ed yesterday, I said, 'Ed, mark
my words . . .' Of course they're spoiling those children,
but you can't make them see that. . . . Well, I didn't say
another word. I didn't even dispute her. I turned and
marched right out of the house. I had hardly got into
the room when the telephone rang and there she was,
saying she was sorry, and that she had spoken hastily
because she was worried. I told her it was all right, but
that I wouldn't take that kind of thing from anybody,
daughter or no daughter. I don't have to. I'm perfectly
independent."

Characteristically, though each might deplore a

shortcoming in one of her own family, no criticism of that family was tolerated in the other. "Oh, that's because you don't really know Bernice. She never was one to make a fuss in public. But she doesn't select a piece of chintz for a bedroom curtain that she doesn't want me to go along to give my opinion."

Side by side, then, with their favourite boast of their own independence was the mythical belief in their families' dependence on them. "The children say it's all right for me to live here alone in the hotel during the winter, if I insist. But in the summer nothing will do but that I've got to be with them, wherever they are." For years, Mrs. Hanauer declared, her daughter's family had gone to the mountains because she, Mrs. Hanauer, could not stand the sea air. Mrs. Grimm, with her son's family, spent the summer months at the seashore because the mountains were bad for her heart.

The hotel apartments of the two women were in the same section, though Mrs. Grimm's was five floors higher than Mrs. Hanauer's, and costlier. She was the more moneyed. Sitting room and bedroom of each presented a bewildering diversity of tastes and periods. Some hotel furniture, some saved from their own housekeeping days, some selected by the smartly modern daughter or daughter-in-law. Before their widowhood each had lived in one of those narrow high-stooped houses that line New York's side streets. From these days each had cherished certain pieces of furniture or bric-à-brac grimly Victorian in mould. Relics, Mrs. Hanauer's daughter called them, of the brown stone age.

These were likely to be fat armchairs once dressed

like portly dowagers in plush, now rejuvenated and simpering in the flowered ruffles of gay-p..tterned chintz. A gloomy and hideous lamp-base of the gnarled nineties was topped by a silk shade palpably representing the Madison Avenue taste of a young matron. The whole gave the effect of an old hag tricked out in a garden hat.

There were pert pillows, gay hangings, colourful book-ends quarrelling with dyspeptic old vases and disgruntled desks. A costly and beautiful toilet set of enamel reposed on the broad bosom of a hopelessly old-style bureau. All these odds and ends mingled in a kind of discordant harmony, through which ran the motif of comfort. A Vernis-Martin cabinet, curtained in green, displayed when opened an array of china and silver rather surprising when one remembered that these were non-housekeeping hotel apartments. Mrs. Hanauer or Mrs. Grimm would hasten to explain.

"I never do any cooking in my room. I wouldn't bother. I'm at the children's two nights a week. They'd make me come every night if I would, but I won't. I have these things because I like to feel that I can make myself a cup of tea without sending downstairs for it. Besides, the stuff they send up! Boiled straw, my daughter-in-law calls it."

The visitor, surveying the chop plates and vegetable dishes and saucers, said—of course.

On the dresser in the bedroom and on the mantel in the sitting room were silver-framed photographs of infants. Mrs. Hanauer and Mrs. Grimm always called attention to these. "My grandchildren!"

"How lovely! How old are they?"

"Let's see. Junior is fifteen and Sister is going on twelve——"

"But then these pictures must have been taken years ago! They're babies!"

"Oh, yes. They're old pictures. But I like them better than the new ones. I always think of them as babies. They were the cutest babies I ever saw, if I do say so."

"Cuter than your own were?"

"Oh, Ed was the ugliest, blackest little thing you ever saw, and cried day and night. Time I was a bride they didn't know all about babies before they were married. Nowadays girls of sixteen know things a midwife wouldn't talk about."

This last speech could have been uttered only by Mrs. Grimm. She prided herself on her modern outlook, but the truth was that her attitude toward that much-discussed menace known as the younger generation bristled with indignation. In this, as in many other points, she differed from Mrs. Hanauer. Tiny, dark, nervous, you thought of an intelligent little simian as you saw her quick movements, heard her scolding chatter, watched the darting venom of her deep-set black eyes. Despite her years Mrs. Grimm's hair had remained stubbornly black except for a reluctant strand here and there at the temples. Her eyebrows, too, were dark and vigorous. This, with her sallow colouring, gave to her a formidable look at variance with the almost childlike smallness of her frame. Quick-tempered, arrogant, she was like a little black-and-tan terrier as she snapped her disapproval.

"Look at that girl! I'll wager she hasn't a stitch on

except that slimsy dress and her step-ins. It's disgusting!"

"I think it's grand," Mrs. Hanauer would say.

"What's grand about it, I'd like to know!"

"Oh, healthy—and kind of cute." Helplessly.

"Honestly, Sophy Hanauer, sometimes I think you're not quite bright."

Mrs. Hanauer did not resent this. In fact, her next remark might have been considered quite irrelevant. Certainly the bristling Mrs. Grimm so considered it. What Mrs. Hanauer said was, "I don't like being an old woman any more than you do."

Sophy Hanauer was what is known as easy-going; a delightful quality. Though slightly older than her friend, she actually looked younger by ten years. This, paradoxically enough, in spite of her white hair. Plump cushions of fat comfortably upholstered her generous old frame. Her skin had been lovely in her girlhood and still was fine and soft. She was not above using a dash of rouge to heighten the effect of her white hair, of which she was very proud. She was quite finicking about the bluing in the rinsing water when she had her hair shampooed at the Beth Beautye Shoppe on Broadway near Seventy-fourth.

Her son-in-law called her the Sport. He was fond of telling his friends a characteristic story. Mrs. Hanauer, one winter, repaid social obligations by giving a dinner for eight at her hotel. The guests were women of her own age, widowed, many of them, well dressed, priding themselves on their modernness. "Tell you what, Sophe," her genial son-in-law had said, "I'll mix a bunch of cocktails and send them over before dinner, see. Start the girls off right." Mrs. Hanauer liked a cocktail with the best of them.

"Oh, they!" she now said, with infinite scorn. "It's no use passing cocktails to them. They've all got high blood-pressure." Jo had roared at this.

"Listen, Sophy," he would often say, to her infinite delight, "if this daughter of yours was half the sport that you are I'd look forward to old age without a quiver."

Mrs. Hanauer and Mrs. Grimm were but two of many well-to-do elderly women living their days in the comfortable, care-free atmosphere of the hotel, with its red-carpeted corridors, its liver-coloured marble lobby, its flat-footed old waiters, its reluctant lifts. They enjoyed complaining about the food in the dining room. Yearly they announced their decision not to renew the lease. Often they spoke of going abroad for a year or more "only the children need me." On rainy days, and during the raw winter months, it was pleasant not to be obliged to go out for company or recreation. Almost any afternoon or evening the quiet of the wide bright corridors was broken by the rattle and clack of mah jong tiles. Through open transoms you heard spoken the poetic or absurd terms of the game. One bam! West wind. Four flowers!

They called each other on the telephone, often addressing one another by the last name only. Coming from them, it produced a racy and piquant effect most startling, and faintly flavoured with rowdyism. "Hello! That you, Hanauer? What are you doing?"

"Oh, I've got some mending——"

"Let it wait. Mrs. Renner is here. I thought we'd have a game if you don't mind playing three-handed."

Their days were very full. They were meticulously manicured at the Beth Beautye Shoppe. They went to the matinée. They went to the theatre occasionally in the evening. They attended symphony concerts. They heard the lectures given under the auspices of the League for Sociological Instruction, of which organization they were members. Here, English novelists and English university professors and English editors spoke with bright insultingness and an Oxford accent on the subject of money-mad, materialistic America, following which speech they hurriedly collected their fee and scurried on to Chicago, there to eject another mouthful of cultural spittle into the eager faces of the members of the Pantheon Club. They read the new books and discussed them. Theirs was the sprightly intelligence of the American middle-class old lady, alert, eager, curious. A strangely youthful buoyancy was expressed in terms of beige silk stockings and smart hats and modish jewellery and jersey sports costumes. They were dignified but snappy.

Twice a week they dined with the children. They endeavoured not to criticize what they considered the extravagance of the household of which they were guests. Yet sometimes they could not resist it.

Strawberries, h'm? In January! My goodness! Somebody must get an awfully big housekeeping allowance. They said, as Ed or Jo carved generous portions of the roast, "If that's for me I only want half of that."

They invited the children to dinner. "But, Mother, how foolish! We're housekeeping. It's so much easier for you to come here."

"I am here twice a week. You haven't had dinner with me in over a month now."

"But there's four of us, and only one of you."

"A person would think I was a beggar. I wouldn't ask you if I couldn't afford it. I'm perfectly independent."

And so they were. Financially independent. Physically active. Socially interested. Equipped to provide themselves with entertainment, stimulus, companionship, a home, clothes, food. Dependent on their children and grandchildren only for that one thing without which they could not live. Love. Human affection.

It was, curiously enough, after one of these family dinners that both Mrs. Hanauer and Mrs. Grimm learned of a change in the children's usual plans for the summer. Perhaps it was not, after all, so strange. Their grandchildren were tall, slim, athletic boys and girls. They thought of them still as babies. Their children were nearing middle age, with graying hair, and with little sudden fans of wrinkles at the corners of the eyes when they smiled.

They regarded them as children not nearly grown up and needing advice and guidance still. And these children, perhaps because of that very independence of which they so often heard the boast, failed to realize that old age, after all, had really overtaken this courageous, keen, and dominating figure whose presence so often brought discord into the household.

They talked it over, husband and wife. It isn't fair to the children. After all, she's as strong as any of us. Twice the energy I've got, if you ask me. Last summer Junior and Sister couldn't stir from one to three because she was lying down. Almost grown-up now, really. Little parties—their friends over in the evening. You can't expect them to act like babies any more. Entitled to their freedom. After all, we're attentive all winter. No one can say we're not. But we've got to consider the children first, I should think.

So then, summer in the offing. The handsome houses in the East Fifties and Sixties began to be boarded up. You sought the shady side of the street. The English culturists took their American dollars home to idealistic Europe. The plays by Molnar and Shaw and Ibsen and Werfel and O'Neill melted before the hot sun and in their place came the cool vapidness of the musical shows.

"Mother"—Mrs. Grimm's daughter-in-law speaking, rather hurriedly, and not looking at her husband—"Ed's hay fever was simply terrible last year, and the cold that Junior had all through August, that hung on so, wasn't a cold at all, but hay fever, too. I suppose he's inherited it."

"Fiddlesticks!" said Mrs. Grimm.

Her daughter-in-law compressed her lips. Then she opened them and spoke still more quickly. "Doctor Borsch said that the pine air is what they both need. In fact, he insists upon it. I'm afraid we'll simply have to go to the mountains this year. Now, you know perfectly well we'd be delighted to have you come along if you think it would agree with you. We're going quite high up. To Kendall's. The cottage is small, but perhaps you wouldn't mind a day-bed in the . . . or maybe a room at the inn near by, and your meals with us. Cook has promised to go along. . . . Joan has asked two of her friends for July . . ."

"Nobody," replied Mrs. Grimm, with terrible distinctness, "nobody has to put themselves out for me. Nobody ever has and nobody ever will. A person would think I was a child. I don't know what I may do this summer. I may go abroad."

From Ed, quickly, "I wouldn't hear of your going to Europe alone."

"Who said I was going alone! I can always hire somebody, for that matter. I'm perfectly independent."

"Now, Mother, don't talk like that. You know how Ed and I——"

"Yes; I know," said Mrs. Grimm.

Mrs. Hanauer's daughter, too, wore the double frown of worry between her eyes. "You know how pale and listless Dorothy was all last summer. Well, Borsch says that what she needs is the ocean air and salt bathing. It's only two hours from New York. It'll be wonderful for Jo. He can come out every Friday and stay till Monday. During August, when it's slack, he might even make it on Thursday. Just think, after all these years of having to take a sleeper overnight to get to us in the Adirondacks. I know the sea air doesn't agree with your bronchitis, but I've just got to consider the children, and Jo."

"Nobody," said Mrs. Hanauer, not unkindly, "has got to consider me." One forefinger was making little circles, round and round, on the arm of her chair; round and round. "A person would think I was a child."

"Don't say that, Mother. It isn't fair. You know we've always loved having you with us, summers. There's room for you. Dorothy can share——"

"I don't know what I shall do this summer. I may go to Europe."

"I wouldn't hear of your going alone."

"Did I say I was going alone? I have plenty of friends, goodness knows, who go every year and who've begged me to come with them, time and again. For that matter, I could hire a companion. I'm perfectly independent."

Neither would confess to the other the true state of affairs. Mrs. Hanauer lied grandly to Mrs. Grimm. Mrs. Grimm was bristlingly offhand to Mrs. Hanauer. I'm sick of the seashore. I'm tired of the mountains. The same people you see all winter in the city. What's the change! A little air. What's that!

"Why don't you try the mountains, for a change?" asked Mrs. Hanauer.

"They don't agree with me. My heart. Why don't you go to the seashore?"

"The doctor forbids it. My bronchial tubes."

They eyed each other for a moment with wary unconcern. Mrs. Grimm spoke first, her tone casual to the point of airiness, "I'd go to Europe, only I don't want to go alone, and there are very few people I'd travel with."

"How about me?" suggested Mrs. Hanauer, with heavy jocularity.

"Are you joking, Hanauer?"

It was arranged. They had both been abroad before, in the days of the defunct Grimm and Hanauer; Mrs. Hanauer only once, Mrs. Grimm many times. Grimm, big, blond, personable, had been an importer; and she had accompanied her husband on his frequent foreign trips with a persistence that savoured more of suspicion than of fidelity. He had, in fact, been known to come home at five with the announcement that he was sailing next morning at ten. Whereupon Mrs. Grimm, looking strangely like Rosa Dartle, would pack a hurried trunk, leave the boy Ed in care of the capable *fräulein*, and steam triumphantly away with him, for all the world like an impish little gnome who has a dejected giant in her power. "I have crossed," Mrs. Grimm would tell you on the slightest provocation, "thirty-six times. In fact, I feel as much at home in Paris or London as I do in New York."

She was inclined to patronize the less cosmopolitan Mrs. Hanauer. For that matter, her manner toward her friend frequently was tinged with some spaciousness. Mrs. Grimm had always had money. She was inclined, therefore, to be prudent to the point of parsimony. Mrs. Hanauer, on the other hand, had the gay lavishness of a child with a bag of lollipops. She had known struggle. Hanauer had bought real estate, but it was as though his name on a deed of sale brought blight to that property. Did he buy east the dwellers fled west as though from a pestilence. He bought north, and progress marched south.

Suddenly, after his death, tumble-down buildings and vacant lots near the East River, left by him to his

widow, a source of no revenue, bloomed Aladdin-like
into twenty-story studio buildings, with ninety-nine-
year leases, and Mrs. Hanauer began buying her hats in
Fifty-seventh Street. Struggle and disappointment had
not embittered her. They had, on the contrary, given
her a racy sweetness and tolerance. "What's the diff!"
she used to say. "You only live once." As though she
had discovered a great truth.

"'At a girl!" her son-in-law would shout. "'At a good
sport!"

Their preparations for the journey were simple. In
their well-ordered lives there was no need for sudden
rush and flurry. Mrs. Grimm was full of travel maxims.
"Go with empty trunks and come back with full ones.
. . . Take enough American silk stockings. Those over
there you can't wear once, even . . . Comfortable shoes,
if you don't take another thing . . . Your own coffee.
This stuff on the boat is like licorice . . . Sunny side of
the deck—heavy coat—American money . . ."

They had two cabins, with a bath between, at a really
outrageous cost. "Travelling like a couple of prima
donnas, that's what you girls are," Mrs. Hanauer's son-
in-law said jovially. Certainly the appearance of those
cabins, at departure, verified his remark. Flowers, books,
candy, fruit, telegrams.

"Why do people do it!" Mrs. Grimm exclaimed,
making a little sound of disapproval between tongue
and teeth. "What a waste! Look at this enormous
basket from Mr. Grimm's ex-partner." She surveyed
Mrs. Hanauer's less imposing floral edifices with a
patronizing eye. A small buttons staggered in with a

structure of fruit that might have lasted the Noah family their voyage. "Grimm?" inquired the lady of that name.

"Hanner or Hanor or——"

"Hanauer," said the genial Sophy, not without a tinge of complacency. "My, look at the size of those pears! A meal in itself."

"Those big pears are generally hard. I don't know why people do it. I always said to Mr. Grimm, the thirty-six times we crossed, if people would only send telegrams, and that's all, how much more sensible."

"I like it," said Mrs. Hanauer. Her voice held a little excited note, like a child's. "I think it's grand. It makes me feel so popular."

"It's an old story to me," remarked Mrs. Grimm.

They stood at the ship's rail as she drew warily out into the bay. Waving up at them from the dock were daughter, son, daughter-in-law, son-in-law, grandchildren. Their faces were round white disks turned toward them in space. To the two at the rail those disks were their world; their solar system; their symbol of achievement in life; their living connection with Life itself.

Write, now! Cable as soon as you land. Don't forget! Take care of yourself! Final futile clutchings into the space that was widening between them. Suddenly the little sallow black-eyed face at the rail and the plump pink blue-eyed face at the rail, side by side, broke into grimaces that were absurd and yet not funny. The white disks swam in a blur.

Mrs. Hanauer's daughter Bernice clutched her husband's arm. The fingers of the other hand were closed over her mouth, in a tight fist, like that of a child who is fearful. "Oh, Jo, she's crying! Look! I don't think we should have let her go. I don't know—she looks so—so —kind of——"

"Oh, now, Bernie, she's all right," said Mrs. Hanauer's son-in-law briskly. "She's a good sport. She'll have a swell time. Person'd think you were the mother and she the daughter, the way you carry on."

Mrs. Grimm's son Ed, his face turned up toward that wizened dark face so strangely contorted at the rail, suddenly set his teeth so that a white ridge sprang out along either side of his jaw. He fumbled foolishly with his hat in his hand.

"Look, Stell! She's crying. I don't know. Do you think we ought've let her go like that, alone? She looks so—so——"

"She isn't alone, stupe! What's the matter with you! You know, Ed, I've always said that you had a mother complex. You spoil her."

They were splendid sailors, both of them. Three meals a day—four for Mrs. Hanauer who liked her tea and cakes in the afternoon.

"I never touch tea on board," Mrs. Grimm declared, bristling, as though there were some special virtue in this abstinence.

Close as their friendship had been, they had never known the irritating intimacy that comes with travel. Mrs. Hanauer was the kind of person who does not screw the top tight on the tube of tooth paste. A sticky white worm usually ornamented the wash-bowl. Mrs. Grimm was the sort of person whom this infuriates. Both women awoke early and had their breakfast in their rooms, but while Mrs. Hanauer rose, dressed, and went out on deck, Mrs. Grimm remained in bed until noon.

"The day's long enough," she said. "Besides, what a chance to rest. Nobody who's used to travel goes galloping around a boat at this hour of the morning."

Their breakfast trays were a startling point of contrast. In one bright little cabin you saw the plump and ruddy Mrs. Hanauer propped comfortably among her pillows, protected by a baby-blue challis bed jacket, a dish-laden tray on her knees, blandly consuming a meal such as that with which a Kansas farm-hand starts his day. The least of its items were the two cups of coffee with excellent cream from the private stock which had been one of the many boat gifts sent them. Mrs. Grimm, hearing her give the order to the somewhat astounded stewardess, would sniff with disapproval. She would state her order in a tone whose every shade was a reproach. Coffee, hot water, dry toast.

"My!" called Mrs. Hanauer from her room, as she deftly applied a quarter of a cube of butter to a hot roll, embellished this with an amber crown of orange marmalade, and popped the whole between her lips, "my goodness, Grimm! No wonder you're so skinny."

The swart little Mrs. Grimm, in bed, was a fly-speck in a pan of milk. The sound of Mrs. Hanauer's bath annoyed her. Mrs. Hanauer was one of those musical bathers. "Will you kindly shut the door, Mrs. Hanauer! I didn't close my eyes all night. I might get a few minutes' sleep this morning if I had the chance."

As they sat on deck side by side, swathed in rugs, relaxed, contemplative, they could not but betray in their conversation something of the hurt which son and daughter had dealt them. Little vague remarks, spoken almost unconsciously, after a long silence, as though the speaker were thinking aloud; phrased incompletely. Well, I suppose that's life . . . You spend your life bringing them up, and then when they don't need you . . . A daughter is a daughter all her life, but a son is your son only until he marries . . . Oh, I don't know about that. I sometimes think my son-in-law Jo is more considerate of me than my own . . . They need me a whole lot worse than I need them, I can tell you.

They would catch themselves, and eye each other warily, stiffening. They would fall to commenting jocosely on their fellow passengers tramping the decks in parade. There was a certain type of old lady encountered on the boat, and later in their continental travels, that aroused their mirth and contempt. These were the frumpy genteel type, the old conservative American family type, or the English gentlewoman in historic hats, black, cloth-topped, buttoned high shoes, black garments of excellent material and bunchy cut. These were attended, usually, by a defeated-looking maiden daughter or a crushed companion. They walked timorously, under sunshades. The sight of them seemed to release something impish in Mrs. Hanauer and Mrs. Grimm.

"I think I'll have my hair bobbed when I get to Paris," Mrs. Hanauer would announce. "Bernice says she thinks it'll be becoming."

"Don't be a fool! Look at that woman, will you! June, and she's wearing black spats. Black spats always make me think of undertakers. I'll bet she's old family, all right." Mrs. Grimm would survey her own small trim foot in its smart patent-leather slippers and cut-steel buckle. She was vain of the size of her foot for some obscure reason that people have for being proud of a member which is built merely in proportion to the rest of the body.

London, Paris, Deauville, Frankfort, Brussels, Lucerne. Theirs was a terrific energy. It was as though, now that the sands were running so fast, so fast, they begrudged the time lost in sleep, in repose. They would sleep long enough, they thought, secretly, and pushed the thought from their minds. They seldom retired until after midnight, read in bed, were wide awake at six. They lay there, thinking, Mrs. Grimm in her room, Mrs. Hanauer in hers. More than three-score years of life lay behind them. They thought of yesterday, and of to-day, but never of to-morrow.

And they quarrelled. Their bickering was almost constant. Perhaps, in the closeness of their companionship, each saw herself constantly reflected in the face of the other. To each other they would not confess to being tired, sleepy, nervous, lonely, travel weary—to any of the quite natural sufferings of sight-seeing. They found fault with one another. They complained of each other, privately, to chance friends or acquaintances encountered in hotel lobbies, on trains, in the parks or shops.

Mrs. Hanauer's magnificent appetite was a source of increasing annoyance to the bird-like Mrs. Grimm. Certainly Mrs. Hanauer, large, placid, amiable, liked to eat. She ate lobster, sweets, cucumbers, acids; liked a glass of mild white wine at dinner. She consumed the four or five courses of the European midday lunch, topping it off with cheese and fruit. Always you heard the crackle of a surreptitious paper bag in her room, after she had gone to bed.

Mrs. Grimm would regard her bristling, tight-lipped with disapproval. "You know you can't eat lobster. Why do you order veal when you can't digest it! Nobody can digest it. My daughter-in-law won't have it in her house. Mark my words, you'll be sick. Don't come to me complaining if you are. If you do get sick who'll have to suffer for it!" A rhetorical question, certainly.

Mrs. Hanauer would survey her in mild surprise. "Why, I will."

"You! No!" Mrs. Grimm would retort. "I will! I'll have to take care of you."

"Nobody has to take care of me, Mrs. Grimm. I'm perfectly independent."

Now that each leaned so hard on the memory of the children in America they perforce denied their dependence on each other.

They confided in such friends as they met on their journeyings. "I hope I can stand it until September," Mrs. Grimm would say to a chance New York friend. "But my patience is nearly exhausted. It has taught me a lesson, I can tell you. My son and daughter-in-law begged me to come to the mountains with them this summer, but I thought a change would do me good. Well, live and learn."

The easy-going Mrs. Hanauer complained in gentle wonderment. "She makes such a fuss about everything. She quarrels with everybody; porters and waiters and chambermaids and people at the railway stations. I honestly am looking forward to the day we sail in September. We'll be home September tenth. I wish it was to-morrow. My daughter insisted that I come with them to the seashore, but I thought I'd come to Europe for a change. It was a mistake. You never know a person till you travel with them, I always say."

Mrs. Grimm's cosmopolitan knowledge was always being flaunted in Mrs. Hanauer's mildly resentful face. "You over-tip. They're not used to it. Anybody who has ever travelled wouldn't tip like a drunken sailor. They only take your money and despise you for it."

"What do I care if they despise me! I want my comfort. If an extra few cents at the end of the week means I get hot water with my tea and an extra pillow and two clean bath towels, what do I care what they say about me in the back hall! I don't want to live with them."

"They only laugh at you."

"Let them laugh, poor things. If they can laugh for fifteen cents I'm glad to furnish the money."

"It isn't the money. It's the principle of the thing."

Sometimes you saw them returning from an afternoon's sight-seeing, walking not together but one behind the other, sulkily, like naughty children.

True to the nickname bestowed upon her by her son-in-law, Mrs. Hanauer, the Sport, loved to gamble. She rarely won, but her glee when she did was out of all proportion to her winnings. In the French watering places, nightly, after dinner, she would scurry to the Casino, there to throw her francs into the omnivorous green maw of the roulette table. She shivered delightfully with the curious tension of excitement that hovers, almost a palpable form, above and around the gaming board. She became quite chummy with the weird, exotic creatures manacled from wrist to elbow with incredible diamond bracelets. Sometimes these borrowed money of her—pathetic sums—fifty francs—twenty—ten, even. The light from the huge crystal chandeliers that hung like frozen fountains above them sent a hundred glorious ruby and amber and blue and orange lights darting from these jewels as the white arms were thrust forward to place a disk on the red, on the black, on the seven, on the eleven.

Mrs. Grimm rarely played. "I've seen too much of it in my life," she said boredly. "It doesn't interest me. Mr. Grimm used to win five hundred francs one minute and lose it the next. That was when five hundred francs meant something." Sometimes she refused even to accompany Mrs. Hanauer on her night's revelry. "Do you know who that woman was you were talking to last night at the Casino, next to you? A woman I met in the lobby just told me. That was that Madame Bey Khan, or whatever her name is—that Frenchwoman who married the Turk, or something, and murdered him in a London hotel. The papers were full of it."

"I thought she looked sad for a woman so young," said Mrs. Hanauer pityingly.

"Well, I've got something better to do than run to casinos and talk to murderesses."

"What?" inquired Mrs. Hanauer bluntly.

"What what?" demanded Mrs. Grimm, bewildered.

"What better to do?"

"Oh, all right. Only when you get sick from nervous indigestion, eating all kinds of things a horse couldn't stand, and then working yourself up over winning a few francs, who'll have to pay for it, I'd like to know!"

Pathetically enough, it turned out to be Mrs. Grimm who first fell ill. There had been some mistake about the train from Frankfort to Brussels. At the last minute they found themselves on the ten-twenty-six, which was not their train, instead of on the ten-thirty-six, which was. Their trunks, too, and innumerable bags were aboard. They discovered this in one panic-stricken minute before the train would have carried them heaven knows where.

There followed the cacophony which attends the making of a mistake in a foreign railway station. Porters, passengers, station agents; shouts, screams, arms waving, luggage hurled, imprecations shouted. Cologne! But we thought it stopped at Cologne. That's the border. We have to change at the border. Which one is it, then? Where is it? We have to get off. Let us off! We're American citizens.

They were off the wrong train and on the right one. Their faces were dully red, with a thick purplish colour. Their foreheads were damp. They were trembling. At last they found seats in a first-class compartment and sank down, spent, their eyes looking strained.

An hour later they could joke about it, feebly. They could even go into the dining car and eat some of the hot and steaming meal with which the European train bombards its passengers. Thick bilious soup. Veal. Greasy potatoes. Stewed and mysterious greens. Salad. Cheese. Fruit. Mrs. Grimm essayed to eat the salad, the cheese, the fruit; wherein she made her mistake. The terror and excitement of the past hour had set all the nerves a jangle in the little frame. Arrived at the hotel, their journey's end reached, she was seized at midnight with the stabbing jagged pains of ptomaine.

"I won't have a doctor. I wouldn't have one of these foreign doctors near me. They almost killed Mr. Grimm, once. In Vienna, too. Of all places."

"Now, Fanny, don't be silly. You've got to take something."

"Castor oil and bismuth. That's all they give for ptomaine. That's what it is. Ptomaine. I told you I didn't want to eat on that train, and you nagged me and nagged me, and so I ate something. Oh!" The little face on the pillow was wizened, green.

"I'll send a boy for it. There must be somebody awake in this hotel. It's only a little after twelve."

"Your bare feet. You're walking around in your bare feet. You'll catch your—oh!" She drew herself into a knot of agony.

Finally at the door, a red-eyed waiter ridiculously formal in a dress suit. No, he could not go. No, there was no one to send. It was after midnight. The chemists' shops were closed, naturally. He did not know. He did not know. He did not know. The dark eyes in the face on the pillow were glazed with pain.

"I'll go," said Mrs. Hanauer. "I'll get somebody up. My God, when you think of all we did for them in the war." A skirt over her nightgown. A coat over this.

"Your hat," gasped Mrs. Grimm, the stickler. "Hat!"

"Hat hell!" said Mrs. Hanauer; and returned twenty minutes later with a bottle of castor oil, an orange, a spoon, a packet of bismuth. Hold your nose while you swallow it. Now wipe out your mouth with this towel. Suck a piece of orange. Bismuth now, and again in the morning. Mrs. Hanauer was up most of the night, thudding across the floor fearfully to gaze at the shrunken and wattled face turned so gratefully, so wistfully up to hers. Yes, you've got a little bit of fever, maybe. But by morning you'll never know you were sick.

"Put on your shoes," moaned Mrs. Grimm, outraged. "Go back to bed."

But twenty times during the night the bare feet thudded anxiously across the floor.

Next morning Mrs. Grimm was weak, but had only occasional and slight pain. By afternoon she was sipping warm milk. Her eyes were sunk deep in her head, but the black lines which pain had etched in her face had vanished. By evening Mrs. Hanauer was sniffling suspiciously. Next day Mrs. Grimm was crawling about, feebly, to administer hot-water bags and aspirin and hot lemonades to the bronchial and wheezy Mrs. Hanauer.

There followed a week of a sort of happy wretchedness, in which each ministered tenderly, unselfishly, to the other.

"You don't need to do anything for me, Fanny. I'm all right."

"Honestly, Sophy, sometimes I think you're not quite bright. If your cold turns into pneumonia who'll have to suffer for it!"

"You will," retorted Mrs. Hanauer unexpectedly, and cackled a hoarse bronchial laugh.

They were sailing from Cherbourg. By the time they reached Paris they were a markedly changed pair, these two who had started out so blithe and independent. Yet still so unchanged. For though they leaned heavily on each other for support, both spiritual and physical, how consistently they refused to admit it.

"You're not fit to go shopping alone. Look at yesterday! If I hadn't pulled you back, that taxi would have run over you the next minute."

"A person would think I was a farmer to hear you talk. I guess if I can get around in New York I can get around in Paris. I knew Paris before you ever heard of it."

The city's bewildering, frantic street life swirled and eddied all about them. They leaped from curb to curb like harried hares. Oh, well, I'm sick of shopping, anyway. I've got the dress for Bernice, and the handkerchiefs for Jo, and the bracelet for Sister and the field-glasses for Junior. I guess they'll have to be satisfied with that.

Weary, but undefeated. Heads bloody, but unbowed.

The children were on the dock to meet them. Son and

daughter-in-law, daughter and son-in-law, they kissed these with a happy perfunctoriness. But the grandchildren they kissed with rapturous devouring kisses, folding them hungrily in their arms.

Please don't stand around me like that while the inspector looks over my things. It makes me nervous. No, Ed, don't give him a cigar. It makes them suspicious. No, I have declared everything, I tell you. But anyway, I get nervous.

"What do you mean, I don't look well!" demanded Mrs. Grimm of her daughter-in-law. "I had a touch of ptomaine, but everybody has that in Europe."

"Just the same," declared her son Ed stoutly, "next summer you'll stay with us. I don't want you running around alone in Europe. I don't like it."

"I'd like to know why not!" blazed Mrs. Grimm, the indomitable. "Nobody has to look out for me. I'm perfectly independent."

"Mother!" exclaimed Mrs. Hanauer's daughter Bernice, "you look thin! You've lost weight! Have you been sick?"

"A touch of my old bronchial trouble. Anyway, I was too fat."

"Well, the next time you'll have your bronchitis right with us, at home. I don't like your running around Europe alone."

"Fiddlesticks!" said Mrs. Hanauer. She eyed her daughter with loving severity. "For pity's sake, where did you get that hat! Nobody's wearing turned-down brims. Everything turns up this year in Paris."

BLUE
BLOOD

BLUE BLOOD

Edna Ferber

BLUE BLOOD

DENNY REGAN was (and is) a hog driver and an aristocrat. In order authentically to prove the cerulean hue of the fluid that flows in Denny's veins you will have to know something of Emerald Avenue, where he lives. But Emerald Avenue is only a street in the district called Canaryville. Canaryville is but a small part of Chicago's West Side. And Chicago's West Side is, after all, merely one huge arm of the sprawling many-limbed giant, Chicago.

It would, perhaps, be simplest to tie the whole subject into one neat knot by saying that Denny, Emerald Avenue, Canaryville, West Side, and Chicago are dominated and permeated by that vast Augean acreage known as the Yards. The Yards is Chicago's fond abbreviation for the Union Stockyards.

Three generations of Regans—Old Dennis, who was Denny's grandfather, sixty-eight; Tim Regan, his father, forty-nine; and now Denny himself, twenty—spent their working hours in the Yards. All day long they worked in that Æsopian city, and at night they dwelt and slept within one block of it. Emerald Avenue is just east of Halsted Street. Halsted Street faces the Yards. Tim, the father, and Denny, the son, born and bred within shadow of the Yards, had olfactory nerves as insensitive to its peculiar malodours as were their auricular nerves to the din of the city. Certainly Old Dennis, with half a century of Yards work resting lightly on his fine old shoulders, would have denied that any odour existed. In three generations of Regans the Yards had risen from a bad-smelling joke to the dignity of an institution.

Old Dennis remembered well when the Yards had been outside the city limits, a reedy swamp wherein the croaking of bullfrogs mingled with the grunting of swine. Old Dennis's son Tim and Tim's son Denny had gone into the Yards as inevitably as a scion of the British nobility follows the law of primogeniture. As Old Dennis and Tim had started as hog drivers, so young Denny now followed that odoriferous calling as the first step in the course of porcine knowledge necessary to a true descendant of the house of Regan.

There is no attempting to describe this abattoir of the world. The Yards are—the Yards. But one might essay to convey an idea of Denny, and Canaryville, and Emerald Avenue.

Canaryville is bounded on the north by Thirty-ninth Street, on the south by Fifty-fifth; on the east by Stewart Avenue, and on the west by Halsted Street. No one seems to know why it is so called. The origin of the district's name is lost in the city's fogs. Old Dennis claimed that in past days the prairies thereabouts were full of wild canaries—an explanation which sounds idyllic, but improbable. But the origin of Emerald Avenue's nomenclature was simple enough. On this side of the Regans dwelt the Gallaghers, and on that side the Rourkes.

Emerald Avenue itself resembles a small-town street
more than one to be found in the centre of a gigantic
commercial city. On either side of it two-story frame
cottages are set in little green yards. Hedges of four-
o'clocks wink their eyes at passers-by. There actually
are catalpa trees amidst the grass plots, and forming a
pleasant vista you see an occasional ancient willow
swooping and dipping down the distance like a colossal
old lady in hoops. Lace curtains in the front windows
defy the hot black breath of Chicago's West Side. All
about the street, like scavenger crows, hover grim fac-
tories, smoke-blackened chimneys. tumble-down tene-
ments, waiting to pounce upon its comfortable plump-
ness. Here and there vacant lots, weed-infested, are
grisly ghosts of past prairie days. Sometimes a neighbourhood relic unconsciously traces the history of a
bygone period. A dilapidated red barn just around the
corner with rusty Fords and battered trucks spilling
into the street bears under its sagging cornice the sign:
Sale To-day. 50 mares and horses.

Doc McDermott's old place, as anyone in the district could tell you.

In the midst of this—cool, fresh, almost prim—lies
Emerald Avenue, a little oasis. Most of its houses are
cottages, but an occasional edifice rises almost to the
dignity of a mansion, and then you know that here
has been the dwelling of one of the early packing-house
princes, content in past days to live near the Yards, but
now kinging it over laws and links and gardens in one
of the city's north shore suburbs.

The street is as Irish as its name. Emerald Avenue

dwellers look down with proper pride on those swart workers who live in the district to the west, known as Back Of The Yards. These are largely Poles, Lithuanians, Slovaks, and a few Bohemians. But a staunch handful of Irish of the old guard are still to be found Back Of The Yards and these are as hoity-toity as the Emerald Avenue Irish themselves, owning their homes these many years past and refusing to be ousted by the dark-skinned newcomers contemptuously designated as Hunkies.

It was here, Back Of The Yards, that Miss Norah McGowan lived, the lady oftenest seen with Denny Regan at the Saturday night dances at Fairyland. A quiet, serious-eyed young woman, Miss McGowan, with a Yards lineage as aristocratic as that of young Denny himself. She herself had a good job as stenographer in the Exchange Building at the Yards, not to mention a father, two brothers, three uncles, and numberless male cousins employed in Packingtown, which is the factory section of the Yards.

Miss Norah McGowan didn't in the least mind dancing with Denny. She loved it. He was a divine dancer. Why wouldn't he be! Irish, twenty, slim, and the son of Tim and Molly Regan. But—she didn't in the least mind dancing with Denny. For when you live Back Of The Yards, and yourself are employed in the Yards, and have a father, two brothers, three uncles and numberless male cousins in Packingtown, you are all unaware of that something which so forcibly smites the stranger in Chicago as he nears Halsted Street (and the breeze from the west). Suddenly, almost inevitably, he will throw up his head, sniff rapidly twice, look startled, and say, with emphasis, "What's *that!*"

"What's what?" the native will retort, perhaps a shade defensively.

"*That!* Gosh! Don't you smell it!"

"I don't smell anything . . . but maybe you mean . . . it might be you imagine it's the Yards."

"Imagine! Why, say!——"

"I don't smell a thing," the native Chicagoan will repeat. And then, paradoxically enough, "I like it."

That faint whiff is but a zephyr of Araby, all laden with the scent of myrrh and attar of roses compared to the thing that Denny Regan encountered each week-day morning as, booted and overalled, he flung open door after door of the heavy-laden freight train packed with great two-hundred-pound hogs that had been travelling by day and by night from the farms of Illinois, of Iowa, or far-away Nebraska. It was Denny's job, as hog driver, to usher these porcine guests out into the Bluebeard hospitality of the Stockyards hog pens. Before and after this daily rite he changed his clothes. He often shampooed his hair. He liked to simmer in the steaming benignancy of the inadequate little tub in the Emerald Avenue cottage. But the Yards were part of him; the pores of his skin, the roots of his hair, the nails of his hands, were of the Yards. For that matter, Denny himself, having grown up in the midst of it, was unaware of the breath of the Yards; all oblivious to it, as were his grandfather, his father, his fresh-faced mother Molly Regan—all the members of the Regan household except his sister, the elegant Ellen. And you should have seen her turn up her nose until that feature threatened to be marred by permanent wrinkles.

The elegant Ellen worked in one of the huge offices housed in the People's Gas Company Building on Michigan Avenue, downtown, and she was renegade to the Yards. She called herself Aileen, and brought home to Emerald Avenue stories of high life as lived at the office in the People's Gas Company Building. She tried, too, to bring that elegance into the Regan household, and looked with disdain on the stamped plush parlour set that was the pride of Molly Regan's life, and ridiculed the pieces of tortured china and glass with which Molly decorated the parlour table and shelf.

"What's the matter with 'm?" Molly Regan would demand.

"They're terrible."

"Oh, they are, are they! Well, go and get yourself married to one of the millionaires or whatever it is that clutters up your office that you're always talking about, and then you can furnish your house the way you like it. This is my house."

"I could furnish my own place now, thank you. I earn as much as Pa does, or nearly, for all he's been working in the Yards for God knows how long. I could live in my own flat like some of the other girls do."

Molly Regan's good-humoured red face took on the unaccustomed pallor of white-hot anger. "Try it, Ellen Regan. You let me hear again about living your own life in any flat, other girls or no other girls, and I'll snatch you bald-headed and have your pa give you a whaling, big as you are."

Molly Regan, born in Chicago, had little or no brogue. Sometimes a word slipped out, or a sentence peculiarly Irish in its construction or phraseology. But only Old Dennis, of the lot, spoke with the tongue of the North of Ireland. What a woman, Molly Regan! A hearty, slam-bang, broad-breasted, light-footed creature who had always made life interesting for the quiet, moody, brooding Irishman who was her husband. Perhaps Tim Regan had married a little beneath him, for Molly had been in service over on the South Side. But it had been a lucky stroke for him. A dramatic woman, Molly, with the gift of making the commonplace seem glamorous. There was always a good deal going on in Molly Regan's household. At the dinner table she could tell a sordid story of the neighbourhood—and immediately the incident and the actors in it were coloured with the aspect of romanticism. Molly was not an especially good cook or housekeeper, though when she put her mind to it, she sometimes turned out an amazing mess of dumplings or a triumph of pastry.

It was incredible what she and Tim had done on his thirty-five a week. They owned the frame cottage on Emerald. Ellen and young Denny and the oldest girl Kitty (now married) had had decent schooling; had been fed, clothed. There had been insurance, church tithes, doctor bills. True, the children had started to work at seventeen, or earlier. But there had been, before that, seventeen years of prodigious eating, shoe-scuffings, garment rending. Yet here they all were. And here was the stamped plush parlour set. All this, on thirty-five a week, cannot be accomplished by good management alone. It takes high faith, humour, courage, health, and a belief in fairies.

There were ways. For example, Tim always brought, home the meat from the market belonging to the packing plant in which he worked. Sometimes he followed his own fancy. Usually he asked Molly, "What'll it be?"

Frequently Molly said, "Whatever they've got strikes you tasty." But when she was planning next day's meal she became more explicit. Tim would bring home in a brown-paper packet certain cuts that the average housewife never heard of. The big spicy-smelling butcher shop, with sawdust covering the floor, was just next to the cold room in whose terrible numbing atmosphere Tim worked. Here Tim Regan would buy, perhaps, the succulent tender tips, sometimes called pork tips, for sixteen cents a pound. These, if ever they found their way into the fashionable butcher shops over east, would have brought forty cents a pound as pork tenderloins. He sometimes fancied beef, and bought T-strips very cheap, well knowing that the crafty butcher outside the Yards would have sold the same as beef tenderloin. He brought home bacon nuggets, which are the square chunks cut off the very end of the choicest bacon because they spoil the symmetry of the aristocratic slab. For this he paid twenty cents a pound instead of your forty-four. Molly Regan would cook it with greens or beans or cabbage. It was superb.

Of course Old Dennis, living with them these twelve years past, since his wife's death, and stepping proudly to his work at the Yards daily as he did, contributed to the household's upkeep. A singularly gentle old Irishman, tall, gaunt, silver-haired, with a face amazingly like that seen in pictures of the more abstemious old mediæval monks who have later achieved a saintship. His blue eyes had a wistful other-world look. His job was that of wielding the nine-pound chopper that cut through the ribs of two-hundred-and-twenty-pound hogs. It was a Herculean task.

"I'm as good as ever I was!" boasted Old Dennis. It wasn't true, but they didn't tell him so. Gradually, in the last few years, they busied him with other jobs about the plant. They kept him occupied, happy. Overseer, they said. Dennis, you'd better oversee this, oversee that. You're the expert. The nine-pound chopper had grown heavy for the old arms, after half a century of service. But when important visitors came through he was often called from this or that job over which he was puttering.

"Here's Dennis," they said. "Fifty years with the company. Show them how a real hog chopper does it, Dennis."

He would step to the platform, king on his throne once more. He stood there, poised for a moment, chopper in hand. At his feet, dressed and pink and glistening, the great hog carcasses slid past him on their way to your kitchen. As each came directly in front of him he lifted the chopper high. Down it came through the massive shoulder of a two-hundred-and-twenty-pounder. It was miraculous that he could wield this instrument with such precision. Two ribs made the cut a New York shoulder. Three ribs made it an English shoulder. One and a half ribs made it a picnic shoulder. And when Old

Dennis's eye, in that fraction of a second, measured one and a half, then one and a half it was.

"I'm as good as ever I was!" boasted old Dennis.

But he often took two swings of the nine-pound chopper now, instead of one, to cleave his way through the huge shoulder. "Sure you're as good as you ever were, Dennis," they told him. "You're a wonder."

In his place now you saw a giant Negro, a magnificent ebony creature with great prehensile arms, and a round head, a flat stomach, flat hips, an amazing breadth between the shoulders. From chest to ankles he narrowed down like an inverted pyramid. He raised those arms that were like flexible bronze, and effortlessly, almost languidly, as you would cut through a pat of soft butter, they descended in a splendid arc. Chuck! said the nine-pound chopper. One beautiful epic gesture. The severed meat moved on, one of an endless procession of hundreds, thousands, millions.

"Fifty years an' more I've done that," Dennis would say complacently. "It's no more than play to me. I've bigger things to see after."

Such, then, was the heritage of aristocracy into which Denny Regan now took his natural place.

His own job wasn't pretty. But then, even princes must learn. There is, as has been the plaint of princelings ever since the king business began, no royal road to learning.

Perhaps it should be told you that young Dennis was beautiful—and he would have knocked you down if he had heard you apply the term to him. Denny was a complete throwback to his North of Ireland ancestors.

He had their high cheek bones, and a certain deceptive look of frailty. His eyes were deep sunk and of a peculiar blue-gray, and the whites were very clear, with just a tinge of blue in them, like a child's. He had a dead-white skin, black hair, and heavy black brows that almost met over the bridge of his nose. His lashes were too long, perhaps, shading his eyes so that they imparted to them a mysterious and dreamy look, most misleading and certainly unexpected in a hog driver, but fatal, nevertheless, to feminine beholders. He was not a merry young man, and rarely smiled. Another point in his favour. Women do not love a cut-up.

From the nature of his work, Denny's hours at the Yards were hard and concentrated. His was an eight-hour shift, supposedly, but often his actual working day was much shorter than that. It all depended upon when the hog trains were due to arrive. Monday and Tuesday were always big days. Wednesday was busy, Thursday just so-so, Friday and Saturday almost negligible. Often it was necessary for him to be on the unloading platform at four in the morning, for weeks together. Sometimes a hog train came in shortly after midnight. You were notified. You had to be there, ready, with your tall ash or hickory pole in your hand.

Denny had already been promoted. He was assistant marker. They'd make him marker soon. He didn't mind the work—rather liked it, in spite of the hours, the filth, the rough labour. In detail it can, perhaps, hardly bear description.

Molly Regan was used to a household whose male members went to work at an hour which more favoured wives and mothers would have considered the middle of the night—as often it was. It was one of her boasts that none of her men folks had ever had to go to work breakfastless. The delicious aroma of coffee and bacon might be sniffed in the Regan household at the most incredible hours of the night and morning. In the years of her marriage Molly Regan had got breakfast by kerosene lamplight, by gas light, by electricity. You saw her moving swiftly, deftly about her kitchen, a shapeless figure in her inadequate kimono, the glow of light, the cheerful splutter of bacon, the scent of coffee and her own cheerful red countenance combining to make mock of the black night that pressed its sinister face against the window pane.

"Late nothin'! And late or no late you'll not go out of this house without you've got something hot in your stomach. Sit down, now, and drink this coffee if it scalds you."

Denny was accustomed to the gray-black of the early morning streets. There were in that neighbourhood at that hour many swift figures like his own passing down Halsted Street, disappearing through the old gray stone gate. In the Yards, through the cattle and hog pens, you heard the cry to the gate key men sounding eerily through the blackness. "O-*key*-oh!" they sounded the call now almost a century old. "O-*key*-oh!" Often, early though it was, drovers, buyers, commission men were already astir. You heard the clatter of their horses' hoofs on the pavement as they wheeled toward the pens, and glimpsed them, romantic figures in this day and age, looking for all the world, with their sombreros and long whips, their spurs and boots, like characters in a Western movie.

Down the long lane between the cattle pens went Denny on his way to the unloading platforms. The locker-room shed, which served, too, as a sort of waiting room in rough weather, abutted on the high platform. Here Denny swiftly changed his clothes, taking from his locker the high thick boots, the grimed corduroy pants, the rough coat, the hickory wand. Sometimes he covered this garb with overalls, but not often. What was the use? Nothing could escape the grime, the odour, of the hog cars.

On sharp winter mornings a fire glowed orange and scarlet in the pot-bellied stove in the centre of the rough room, and the drivers, as they waited for their laden train, talked or dozed on the wooden benches. They were, for the most part, lean young fellows like Denny, and largely Irish. Sometimes you saw among them a grizzled veteran who, through inertia, or mischance, or lack of enterprise or fitness, had never risen above the job of hog driver. In mild weather they lounged about the platform or perched on the fence, staff in hand, keeping a sharp eye out for the first glimpse of the puffing black engine coming round the bend. At sight of it they swarmed the platform, took their places. As the train approached, stopped, they pushed open the sliding doors, set the runway, and out poured the flood of squealing, scrambling, slipping, grunting porkers. The noise was terrific. The stench was appalling. The filth oozed under your boots. You prodded with your long hickory stick. You cried, "Soo-ey! Soo-ey!" and stepped nimbly this way and that, and just escaped being knocked down by a great ponderous charging mass of hog flesh. You pulled and tugged as this or that unwieldy bulk refused to take the step from car to runway. "Soo-ey! S-s-s-seeee!" Toward the end you entered the car itself to hasten the laggards. If, in one far end, you saw a mound that lay still and stiff, you and one of the others took hold of it and dragged it out and dumped it on the platform, where it lay stark and, somehow, dreadful, even in the midst of that city of slaughter. For had not the Enemy stolen up and met it halfway even as it came, all unknowing, to the fatal rendezvous.

Train after train. Car after car. Hundreds, thousands, hundreds of thousands of hogs. Food for a nation —for the world, indeed. The stench in his nostrils, the grime in his clothes, the pandemonium in his ears. "Heh! So-o-o! Soo-ey!" called Denny Regan, working with stick and arms and feet. "Sooey! S-s-s-seeee!"

Often by noon his day's work was finished. A change of clothes again (this job of his called for as many changes as a matinée idol's). His time was his own until to-morrow morning. He could go home to Emerald Avenue, there to snatch an hour or two of sleep. The movies. A ball game. The pool shack. The street corner. He was owner of a hybrid car of obscure origin and temperamental moods. You saw many such standing outside the frame cottages on Emerald Avenue, or Union or Wallace near by. Denny's car, or these others, were likely to be embellished with large and flapping muslin posters tacked across the radiator or the gas tank.

"Reëlect Tim Fitzgerald County Commissioner," commanded these posters in large blue letters.

Oddly enough, though it might be noon and her lunch hour, Denny never once thought of meeting Norah McGowan in front of the Exchange Building where she worked, though this was a scant five minutes' walk from the unloading platforms. The boys and girls in the Yards did not consider the lunch hour a time for dalliance. Dates were for hours of relaxation and ease, after the workday was over. She would have been scandalized at the suggestion of their meeting for lunch. Denny liked to be with Norah. She soothed and exhilarated him at once. She was easy to be with. Perhaps he had not concretely thought of marriage with her. He had not thought of marriage with anyone. But the Regans married young and stayed married. There was Norah, of course. Perhaps that was the trouble. There was Norah, dependable, laughing, hearty. And there was, hidden deep, a strong vein of the romantic in this silent, handsome, brooding, moody hog driver.

Denny never was at a loss for something with which to fill his afternoon. Halsted Street saw to that. The many saloons that once had lined that thoroughfare had vanished now, of course. Still, there were places if one cared to use them. Pappy the Greek's. Genzer's Soft Drink Parlour. The Range Cigar Store and Pool Room. Jake's Candy Kitchen. And of course the club rooms. Denny had never run with any of the two or three powerful and sinister gangs that infested the neighbourhood. Political clubs, they were called. Usually they had rooms above some store on Halsted; and police protection. Denny knew them. Tactfully, warily, he steered clear.

Coming into the locker room one May morning, he noticed a new driver. They came and went. You paid little attention to them. This young fellow had a locker next to Denny's. He was, too, about his own age, and undoubtedly Irish, but of the other type; sandy-haired, freckled, stocky, blue-eyed. His shoulders were too broad for his height, giving him a rather simian look, particularly as his arms were long. Still, it was a frank, good-natured face. He had some trouble with his locker key. Denny showed him how it worked. He offered Denny a cigarette. This was not according to hog drivers' ethics. Still, Denny took one. The brand was the same as that which he himself was accustomed to smoke.

"New guy, ain't you?"

"Yeh."

His heavy boots, his corduroy pants, his woollen shirt were new. Denny eyed them.

"Worked in the Yards before?"

"No."

"You want to be careful. First thing you know you're liable to get a spot on them clothes."

"Yeh, I was worrying about that," said the new one. "Give me the address of your dry cleaner, will you?"

"Don't get fresh, guy," Denny warned him.

"Why, say, take a joke, can't you!" The boy's blue eyes bore a look of hurt surprise. And as he spoke he lifted gently out of his way one of the benches that was preventing his locker door from opening to its full width.

It was a bench with solid wooden seat and back and heavy iron legs. On it, at the moment, were two extremely substantial gentlemen in the hog driving profession. He had lifted the bench almost without bending, and much as you would move a book from that side of the table to this. Just a cord in his great short pillar of a neck swelled ever so slightly. "Excuse me," he said, addressing the two on the bench. "I gotta get into my locker."

"That's all right, fella," said one of the two on the bench, palpably impressed. "Leave us know before you get ready to move the shack though, will you?"

Down the track came the hog train. The drivers swarmed the platform. The new man followed, uncertainly. Denny eyed him with a new respect. "Stick with me," he said. "I'll show you."

The new man stuck, gratefully. By noon his boots were as unspeakable as Denny's.

He was a friendly cuss. And he always had a cigarette pack. He and Denny became rather friendly in that remote, unquestioning way men have. He was known as Red. Sometimes, when they had cleaned up, they crossed Halsted to the drug store on the corner (oh, but the street had fallen upon evil days!) and straddling the high stools at the drug store soda fountain had ten minutes' laconic talk as they ate. Gravely and thoughtfully they would order and consume one of the monstrous and sissy messes with which the American male now regales his leisure moments. Their broad shoulders drooped over a miniature mountain of vanilla ice cream with cascades of chocolate sauce, topped by a

snowcap of marshmallow. The white-coated Greek behind the counter seemed to find nothing unusual in pro-
viding such sticky and unadult provender to two power-
fully built males. Sometimes this artless fare was abet-
ted by one of the surprising sandwiches which made up
the fantastic menu printed and pasted up on the mirror.
Veal, ham, spaghetti, salmon salad, cheese-and-slaw.
Denny and Red talked tersely. It was a pleasant enough
place, with almost the comfort and informality of a club
room. Telephone booths, cigarettes, cigars, chewing
gum, candy; a soothing scent of spicy drugs, perfumery,
fruit. A plump impersonal blonde young woman attended to mysterious feminine requests behind the
counter at the far end.

Denny never dreamed of inviting Red to the house on
Emerald. Sometimes, though infrequently, the two went
off together in Denny's makeshift car. They knew very
little about each other. Their talk was a thing made up
almost entirely of monosyllabic words.

From Denny: "You going to stick with the Yards?"

"Sure. You?"

"Yeh. We all been. My old man and his old man and
all. All our life."

"Me, too."

"Yeh! You ain't said before. Right in the Yards, or
what?"

"Packingtown's where I head in. Where my old man
is, and all."

Sometimes they talked of women.

"You running with anybody?"

"Yeh, I got a girl. She lives Back Of The Yards.

Works over in the Exchange Building. She's a good kid, at that."

"What's she like?"

"Well, I don't know. She's a good kid. Easy-going. . . . No, I don't mean what you mean. No, not her. Say, she reminds me of my old woman more than anything, at that. Jolly, and a kidder, and laughing, and don't get sore. Not that you can get fresh with her, see, because I tried it and you can't."

"Figuring to marry her?"

"No!" said Denny, hotly, and a little surprised at the vehemence of his own denial. "I ain't figuring to marry anybody."

Red spoke simply. At something in his voice Denny looked up, quickly, and saw the other's features twisted with pain. What Red said was, "My girl turned me down because of the Yards." His round pink face was a deeper pink, and his blue eyes were suddenly dark.

"How do you mean—the Yards?"

"Well, I'm working in the Yards, see, and I can't stay out late much, and like that, because getting up so early and all, a guy can't. But that isn't all. The stuff gets into your skin or something, and it doesn't matter how much you change and bathe and m—uh—bathe. And when we're dancing she says it makes her sick, see. And she wants to know if I'm going to stick with the Yards, and how long this is going to go on, and all, and I tell her years, though maybe later on I won't have a job that smells so bad, and at that she says it's either her or the job."

"Ha!" jeered Denny, and spat. "The nerve of 'm!
Say, I hope you told that jane where to get off at."

"Yeh," croaked Red, miserably. "Yeh, I told her."

"Didn't want you to work in the Yards, huh? Say, I
figure when I get married my kid's going to work in the
Yards like me and my old man and his old man, see?
Only different, see?"

Red, forgetting his own troubles momentarily,
seemed interested. "How's that? How do you mean,
different?"

"Well, I quit school when I was seventeen. My old
man, he quit when he was thirteen. And his old man—
my grampa—he quit when he was ten. Well, my kid,
he's going to have an education in him, and don't you
forget it, and then he's going to start like me in the pig
driving or like that, but when he finishes he ain't going
to have no lousy little job like my old man or like
Grampa after he's been working a hundred years or
better in the Yards. Grampa, he thinks all the old birds
that started Packingtown and made their piles there—
old Cassidy and Martin Madden and like that—are like
the guys in the Bible. What they do is right, see, even
when it's wrong. He's always saying how good they been
to him, and how old Madden, once when he happens
to be in the Yards and sees him, shakes his mitt, see, and
calls him Dennis. You'd think he'd give him a million.
My old man, he's different again. He's in more with
labour, and like that. Always beefin'. At that he's
headed in right, only he don't know what it's about.
Grampa tells him about this meeting up with Madden,
and Pa says, 'Well and all, what of it!'

"'What of it!' Grampa says. 'He shook my hand and called me Dennis, didn't he?'

"Pa laughs and says, 'You worked for him all your life. You give 'em everything you got in you, didn't you? Well!'

"'They paid me for it, didn't they!' the old man says.

"'Like hell they did!' says Pa. At that, he's right. Only he don't know, like I do, that we're what counts now. My kid, he goes into the Yards, see. But he knows where he's headin' in when he goes, like I do. Only better."

The elegant Ellen, hearing something of this new friend of her brother, was languidly curious but contemptuous, too. Each member of the family was likely to encounter, in its work day, certain characters or co-workers that so impressed them as to bring them into the talk that went round at the family supper table. Red said this. I was talking to Red and he said that.

The elegant Ellen's saga was all about a certain young lady named Genevieve who graced the office in which Ellen was employed downtown. The named occurred again and again in the table talk. All the graces, all the amenities, all the elegancies, were embodied in this young lady who, by now, had become a myth (and a jest) in the Regan household. Ellen had once unfortunately explained that the owner of the name insisted on the French pronunciation. She illustrated.

"Jenny-veeyave!" Molly Regan had exclaimed. "Save us all, what a name!"

"It's French," Ellen went on. "Her father was French."

"What's this Jenny-veeyave's last name?" Molly inquired.

"Duppy." Then, hurriedly, as a shout went up, "But that's only because of the way it's pronounced in America. Du Puis, that's what it used to be. Du Puis."

Denny Regan choked vulgarly over his hot coffee. "Listen, did you ever tell her about your swell brother Dennay?"

"She knows about you, all right," was Ellen's rather surprising reply to this.

"What do you mean, knows about me?"

"That Saturday you met me downtown when we went to buy the radio and you were waiting outside. She saw you. She said she thought you were a handsome sheik and she'd like to know you."

Denny Regan, though he affected to be taken very ill on hearing this statement, was as palpably pleased as any male invariably is under like blandishments.

"Why'n't you bring your friend here some time for Sunday dinner, or after work to supper?" inquired the hospitable Molly. "If she lives alone, like you say, with another girl, I bet she don't get any too much to eat."

"Here!" exclaimed the elegant Ellen, with a glance around.

"Leave me know when you do," said the gallant Denny, "and I'll be out."

But he was not out. When the exquisite Genevieve Duppy appeared, Denny was in. Not only in, but having been warned of her coming, was bathed, shaved, lightly powdered, heavily sartorial, silent, magnetic, and less like a hog driver and more like Brian Boru than any youth named Denny Regan has a right to be.

Having, ever since adolescence, been relentlessly pursued by all manner of young ladies drawn by his good looks, his indifference, his silence, or all three, Denny's defenses were all planned for a mode of attack quite different from that now employed by Miss Duppy.

Miss Duppy was dainty. Miss Duppy was cool. She was good. She was elegant beyond words. She was frail, blonde, lymphatic. You, having swept your plate clean, saw with dismay that her fork was mincing fastidiously about among the less gross tidbits that made up her own portion. She leaned toward you a good deal, rarely smiled and almost never when you expected her to; was altogether a thoroughly selfish and charming little defective. All the boys in Ellen's office were in love with her.

She succeeded in making Molly Regan feel a little sorry for her, which, with her equipment, was the most effective thing she could have done. She patronized Ellen. She was more silent than Denny so that, as he took her home (in the hybrid car) he found himself growing loquacious. Her diction and vocabulary were much less elegant and varied than her manner and Gallic background would have led you to expect.

"Can you imagine! . . . I'll say you're wonderful! . . . You slay me! . . . Honest!" all uttered in a small pale voice that made the memory of Miss Norah McGowan's hearty utterances seem Amazonian in comparison.

Did she like to dance? Yeh. Would she go some time?

Maybe. Next Saturday night? Uh, let's see, what's to-night? Call me up.

There began a series of tortures for Denny Regan. This office Borgia delighted in making her victims writhe. Her tricks were cheap, and Denny was deceived by them. She broke engagements, pretended offense when none had been offered, was deliberately provocative and took refuge in false dignity. She made nothing of Denny's none too imposing weekly wage at the Yards. Through it all she disparaged the Yards, said the thought of it made her sick, and was none too delicate in stressing this fact as she danced with the miserable Denny.

Sometimes he encountered the forthright Miss Norah McGowan. "What's the matter, Denny? You sore at me?"

"No."

"I haven't seen you lately."

"I been busy."

As if she didn't know. Miss McGowan's hearty laugh had grown hollow; had ceased.

Denny stood outside the People's Gas Company Building on Michigan waiting for Miss Duppy on Saturday afternoon. He looked, somehow, different from the other boys stationed there at the curb on similar intent. The big office buildings along the Avenue held many Genevieves. Denny's difference lay, perhaps, in the breadth of shoulder, the clearness of skin, the limpidness of eye, the coördination of muscle. Those others were, for the most part, office workers, male counterparts of Genevieve herself. Hog driving is an unromantic but healthy business, and keeps one out in the open air. Perhaps it was this quality—this difference—which after all had attracted the anæmic Genevieve to him in the first place, and which attracted her with increasing strength, so that she now had some difficulty in pursuing her customary tactics by which she was to remain free and solvent while the victim was bound and broke. She found increasing fault with him. He was contrite. She made unreasonable demands. He was abject. She objected to his manners, clothes, conversation, friends, home, address, finger nails. He considered changing them all. He was in love.

She made a mistake. It was one night when he was having Sunday supper in the murky little kitchenette flat which was the home of Miss Duppy and two of her co-workers. The co-workers were out seeking social diversion. She gave him tea and a pallid and abominable dish known as Waldorf salad, a sickly concoction made up of diced apples and nuts and mayonnaise, and rightly despised of all virile males. Denny, bred to the vigorous stews and roasts and greens of Molly Regan's Emerald Avenue ménage, was dutifully consuming this unvital mess and finding it sawdust but ambrosia. The scene was domestic, intimate. Denny looked masterful. Perhaps this natural little parasite sensed in him potential success; saw in him something of the substantial future which was inevitably to be the lot of this serious, quiet, secretly romantic but clear-headed young Irishman.

She made a mistake.

She had dilated upon the aristocracy of her ancestry, the Gallic strain in her blood, the exquisiteness of her lineage. Her folks, she said, lived in a little town in Wisconsin. Her mother was dead, her father had remarried, her stepmother did not understand her. Common, that's what she was. She did not understand Genevieve's love for things that were fine and beautiful.

"And," said Miss Duppy, concluding the tale of her own elegance, "why don't you get a decent job somewheres downtown?"

"What?" said Denny, not as one who has not heard, but as one would ask who has failed to understand.

"Why don't you get a job downtown, like the other fellows I know? You could. If I'm going to keep on going with you I can't have the girls all laughing at me because you're a hog driver. It's terrible. It makes me sick." She shuddered. "The Stockyards. Killing and everything."

"Makes you sick, does it?" inquired Denny, with a quietness that she mistook for meekness.

"Oh, yes," replied Miss Genevieve Duppy, and shuddered again and made a little face.

"Do you mean if I keep on a hog driver and in the Yards you'll quit going with me?"

"Well, yes, of course." Miss Duppy had hardly hoped her victory would be so immediate, so complete.

Denny crushed his cigarette into the midst of the Waldorf salad remaining on his plate, and rose. "Goodnight," he said.

Miss Duppy stood up, too, quickly. "What do you mean, good-night!"

Denny's voice was not lifted above his usual conversational tone. If anything it took on a lower pitch with the passion of his outrage. "Listen, Frenchy. You ain't the only one has got blue blood in their veins, and don't you forget it. Me, I'm the son of a son of a hog driver. My grandfather remembers when they used to dump cattle and hogs on the sand hills outside the city limits and sell 'em for so much a head. That's how far back he goes. My uncle, John Daley, is the champion beef dresser of the world, see. Not of the Yards. The World! Twenty minutes from opening to dropping the hide. We been in the Yards since there was any. My grandfather and my father and me and my kid. You talk about your folks, will you! I guess when it comes to blue blood we're there!"

"What do you mean, your kid?" asked Miss Genevieve Duppy, a little breathless.

"Why—I don't know," replied Denny, foolishly; and thought suddenly of Norah McGowan, who so strangely reminded him of his mother. Suddenly he strode out of the house, down the stairs, into the street. Miss Duppy's laugh, finely dramatic as it was, failed to reach his ears.

There were two people he wanted to see. Miss Norah McGowan. And Red. Red, whose girl had turned him down because he worked in the Yards and was redolent of the Yards. Hurt, angry, indignant, disillusioned. He'd go over to Norah's. Bet she was sore, and no wonder. He'd call up Red first, here in the corner cigar store. Red. Red what? He didn't even know Red's last name.

Norah? Norah was in. Not only was Norah to be found at home in the McGowan house Back Of The Yards, but her mother was home, and her father, one of her two brothers, two of her three uncles, at least five of the cousins, and countless offspring of all these. There was about that family gathering something impressive, hearty, smacking of royalty, so sufficient were they unto themselves, so clannish, so established, so sure.

Denny they greeted as one of them; prince of another such line. Not a word of reproach from Norah. Not a glance of offense from Ma McGowan. Blue Blood. How your ma? How's all the folks? Norah came forward. Her manner was hearty, but perhaps there was just a shade of reserve beneath. Her cheeks were pink, but it was the pink of sudden flush, and not her accustomed ruddy colouring.

"Hello, Norah."

"Hello yourself, Denny."

"Thought you might like to take in a movie or something."

She hesitated just the fraction of a second. "Kind of —late, isn't it?"

His voice dropped an octave, and vibrated. "Aw, Norah, it ain't late."

"I'll get my hat."

Denny, waiting, chatted laconically and easily with the clan. Their interests his, their viewpoint his, their life his. He and Norah stepped out of the warm, odorous, teeming little room into the warm, odorous, teeming city night.

"The old boneyard's certainly hitting it up to-night," said Denny.

Norah lifted her head and sniffed a little, but whether the sniff was one of pride or investigation was difficult to know. "I don't smell anything," she said, a shade stiffly. And at that Denny Regan linked his arm through hers and brought hers sharply against his hard young ribs.

"Me neither," he said.

It was not until next day at noon, over one of the sticky mixtures at the drug store soda fountain, that Denny had a chance to confide his story to Red. Red was all understanding, all attention. Didn't he know! Hadn't he suffered!

"And say," Denny concluded, "after I bawled her out, like that, telling her how I was a son of a gun myself when it come to family, see, why all of a sudden I wanted to get hold of you, see, and spill how I got the same deal from a jane that you'd got. Well, you could have knocked me for a gool when right in the telephone booth I remembered I didn't even know your last name and we been working together months, driving and all. Can you match that for brains! Say, what is your name anyway, Red? First and last."

"Madden," said Red, "Martin Madden."

"Yeh!" jeered Denny. "Mar——" A terrible thought struck him. He put down his spoon so that it clattered on the marble counter. He looked at Red and saw that gentleman's intensely rising colour more than justify his nickname. "Say, listen. You ain't the son of the old— why, say——"

"Yeh," said Red. "Learning the business from the ground up, like you. What's the matter with that?"

"Je's!" said Denny Regan.

THE END